This book is dedicated to God my Father, my Lord Jesus and His precious Holy Spirit. I attribute all that I am to Him. I praise God for all the beautiful and wonderful people He has positioned in my life. I can not name them all, but every man, woman and child who has crossed my path has been a blessing. Even those people that I at one time considered a hindrance were in my life for a reason. Every situation, even those that were painful, has been a source of inspiration.

I Don't Want Your Man,
I Want My Own

BY *ALVEDA KING*

James C. Winston
Publishing Company, Inc.

Trade Division of Winston-Derek Publishers Group, Inc.

TO SOW THE FALLOW SOIL

First printing

PUBLISHED BY JAMES C. WINSTON PUBLISHING COMPANY, INC.
Nashville, Tennessee 37205

Library of Congress Catalog Card No: 92-63256
ISBN: 1-55523-588-3

Printed in the United States of America

Introduction

This book started out as a poem. As I continued to share it with women and men in my daily walk, memories and testimonies began to emerge. Before long, it became apparent that I should write them down because it was all becoming too much of a mouthful for a casual five minute conversation.

This is not one woman's testimony. This is not one man's testimony. This is a collection of testimonies, written in such a way that the names and identities of the contributors are not included. In this way, the contributors are free to share openly in honesty without being concerned with censure.

Every memory in this book is true, with as little exaggeration as possible. Names have been changed out of a respect for privacy. I have saved the happiest testimonies for last because they bring great hope to women who are awaiting God's best for their lives.

If these testimonies help anyone in anyway, then to God be the glory. May His name be praised forever.

I Don't Want Your Man, I Want My Own

Dear Sister, I just sat down to tell you this.
I don't want your man, I want my own.
Not your man, who lies to you about me,
And to me about you, about me.

I don't want your man, I want my own.
Only, it just so happens he's out having some of that stuff
That things go better with . . .
You know, coke. Not the brown sugary drink,
But the white powder that lies almost as much,
If not more than he does.

I don't want your man, I want my own.
Only, he's out somewhere chasing dreams,
Or skirts, or money and other material possessions
That he feels he must have in order to make me

And most of the female population consider him
To be a god.
God help him if the chase lands my man in jail.

Now I know that some sisters get confused,
And because God ordained
That Man should and would have Woman,
Womankind just must have a Man.
Seems like some of the brothers got confused too,
And ended up with their wrists bent.
But God still has a plan.

It must be that since God in His infinite wisdom
Ordained Man for Woman and vice versa,
Then Almighty God must have a plan,
So that I and all the many sisters like me
Can have our own men.

Cause we really don't want your man, we want our own.

I want a man who loves Jesus,
Who reads the Holy Bible,
And who fears Almighty God.
Now, if this description fits your man,
Then he won't want me anyway,
Because he understands God's plan.
If your man is God's man,
Then you're his Good thing that he's found.

This being the case, I sure don't want your man,
I want my own.

So I pray that your man is God's man,
And I rejoice with you, my sister.
I pray that you and your man stay in God's plan.
Now pray for me my sister.
Cause I really don't want your man,
I want my own.

Pray for your man, for my man,
For the man who must find God . . .
So that your sister and my sister won't be after your man,
And my man.
Cause we really don't want your man.
We want God to give us our own.

So we pray that your man will be strong,
Will know God,
Will stand up and be an example for my man,
And every other sister's man.
So that Man can stand up
And be a voice in the wilderness of drugs, crime, poverty,
So that there will be enough of Man to go around.

So that you can have your man,
And I can have my man,
And our sons can learn to be real Men,
So that our daughters can understand
What it is to love a man,
So that God's plan for a real Man will come to be.

Because a woman doesn't really want another woman's man,
She wants God's own.

The Man Of My Dreams

Every woman has a dream or an expectation of the man she desires to spend her life with. Of course, some dreams never come true. Many women become bitter, hurt and disillusioned by relationships and life circumstances to such a point that they forget that their dreams ever existed. As a result, many women become lesbians, prostitutes, drug addicts, workaholics, or follow other courses in life rather than to pursue the dream of being found by a man who is perfectly suitable for them.

Many women do not wait to be found, but rather take matters into their own hands and go after men whom they find attractive. Often, women are able to lead men into relationships and marriages that otherwise would not come to be. For many women, having a man in their lives becomes an obsession, they must have a man at all costs.

Somewhere between obsession and abject loneliness is a healthy relationship. It is very safe and healthy to rest in Jesus while you are waiting for the right relationship to come into your life. It doesn't hurt to dream of a perfect man, if the dream doesn't become an obsession. I'd like to share the man of my dreams with you.

He comes running towards me on the beach; he reaches me, sweeps me off my feet (of course, I'd have to lose about 100 pounds at the time of this writing), and dashes away with me in his arms, straight into the most dark, sinful, iniquitous pit in the world. With me at his side, a Bible in his hand, and the love of God in our hearts, we tackle the hosts of darkness and win many souls to the Lord Jesus!

Please don't confuse this dream with fantasy; it's a heart's desire. The Bible says if we delight ourselves in the Lord, He will give us the desires of our heart. I do desire a mate who is truly strong in God, a man who is equipped to be the priest of our family.

After two marriages and too many relationships with men, I am at the point where I can either wait for the right man, or be happy without a man. Ladies, please understand that it is okay *not* to have a man; it will not kill you. It is God's pleasure that we all have mates, but He will sustain us until He perfects all things in our lives!

Thank God that a man is not the answer to everything in life. Jesus is life's answer to everything that we need, and He has that perfect relationship for us. If we miss the man of our dreams, we have the Lord of the universe to attend to us.

Barbara: Childhood Memories

As a little girl, I had an opportunity to observe all types of relationships between men and women. My immediate family and my extended family was resplendent with the image of marriage and family. Family was a big deal to us. Even the relationships of the friends and associates of the family were all pictures of wonderful marriages and families.

Many of the people that our family associated with were pastors and their wives, and church people. In fact, in the 1950's, living in Atlanta in the heart of the Bible Belt, life was more in the mode of a church community. In general, people did not hang out late, there was no such thing as "acceptable" shacking. Abortion was still illegal. The focus was on family, the church, education.

During my very early childhood, the only male/female relationships I was aware of were either brother, sister, cousin friendships; husband/wife relationships; or boyfriend/girlfriend relationships. My mom and dad were married; my granddad and grandmom were married; my uncle and aunt were married, and my aunt was "courting" in a respectable way.

Just as I was entering my teenage years, I discovered that relationships were not as simple as they had appeared to be during my early years. Beginning in the 1960's, I was allowed to participate in political and social activities as well as continuing my involvement in church activities. As a result, I met more people, in all kinds of situations.

One night, my father came home late from a function and came into the house. Although he was a preacher, he had been drinking, a fact my family tended to cover up and ignore. He came straight into the house, went into his room and went immediately to sleep. My room was near the garage, and I heard a woman weeping. We had an electric garage, and the only way to get out of the garage was to come through the house. The perplexed woman, who had been in my father's car, didn't know what to do, so she sat in the car crying. I went and tried to wake up my Dad. He didn't budge. I asked Mom to take the woman home; she asked me if I was crazy. I don't remember how the woman got home. I never found out why Dad brought her home in the first place.

Another time, Dad took me and my female cousin to a hotel room. Dad was accompanied by another preacher friend of his. They knocked on the door to the hotel room. Two prominent, well known women, one a politician, one the wife of a wealthy businessman, opened the door. The women were dressed in beautiful negligees. Dad threw back his head, laughed, and said something to this effect: "I want you to know what a real lady is, and what one isn't."

I had the opportunity to know the wives and girlfriends of many of my Dad's associates. The wives were expected to pretend that they didn't know the girlfriends existed. These numerous experiences helped me to gain contempt for adultery. I resolved at an early age to never commit adultery. It was deplorable. I didn't

7

know much about the Bible. I had accepted Jesus at age five, but didn't have a relationship with Him. My Granddad, Dad, and Uncle were real Bible preachers, but they didn't preach much out of the letters. Their lessons out of the Gospel were more about God's goodness and amazing grace, rather than the wages of sin. So I didn't understand the spiritual ramifications of adultery, but I knew its devastating effects.

Somehow, though I had contempt for adultery, I didn't hate the "other" women. I would get angry with them; I would resent them, but I always had a desire to understand them, to understand why they would pursue relationships with married men. I didn't understand human nature and human need at that time. I was not involved intimately with men myself. I was a virgin until two weeks before I married my first husband. It's funny, many of my girlfriends were becoming sexually involved with men during the sexual freedom of the sixties. But, thanks to my dad and his mother, my grandmother, I had a pretty clear understanding of sex, that it was made for marriage, and that it was good to wait. Of course, this is the picture that Dad wanted me to have, he didn't explain about affairs and things. He wanted me to be sheltered.

That's why I was so angry when I discovered the double standard. It was okay for the men to have affairs, but not women. I was puzzled at this reasoning. Men would sleep with women, so how were the women to remain pure if the men violated them? In my reasoning, it didn't even matter if the women wanted to be violated. I felt that they were taken advantage of. I was pretty mad at the men, because I felt they were using the wives and girl-friends. As the years progressed, and I married two men who became involved with other women during our marriage, I found myself very angry and intolerant to their adultery. I felt that I was reliving the experiences of my mother and all the other women I knew. But somehow, even though I was very angry with each husband, I never remained angry with the women.

8

I remember talking with my dad just before he died. I was angry with him about the drinking and the adultery. I knew one woman he was involved with very well; in fact she had just left the city. I had seen her at the apartment of my dad's preacher friend, and she had been absolutely hysterical, demanding that Dad leave Mother and his family (three sons and two daughters). I never found out what Dad promised her because he died the next day. As soon as the lady found out that Dad was dead, she called long distance, (she had flown home just after her ultimatum) and she was hysterical. She kept insisting that his death was her fault because she had demanded that he leave Mom. I remember talking to Dad's girlfriend, trying to calm her down, while wondering what my mom would do when she returned from a vacation. I didn't tell the girlfriend that part of Dad's last words to me had been "I will never leave your mother." I didn't even tell her that she wasn't the only "other" one. There was something mean and spiteful in me that wanted to break her bubble, but she was so hurt, so vulnerable that I didn't do it. I knew that Dad must have promised her something, while still holding on to all his promises to Mom. I had even heard Dad tell Mom, "If you ever leave me, I'll kill you."

Soon after, this woman had a nervous breakdown. As the days went by, I had a chance to see many of the women Dad had been involved with, some famous, some pretty, some intelligent, all kinds. Having no spiritual insight, I had no way of knowing that these women had been on satanic assignment. They literally had hell in them, and out of their vulnerability and need, had been used by Satan to bring a "called man" down. Dad had a strong ministry call of God on his life, and women and liquor always warred against that call. I don't think Dad or any of his associates had a real understanding of this destroying force. Today, I know that Dad and all men are just as much victims as the women are.

In the war of the flesh, if a person is not equipped by and with the Spirit of God, he or she is open game for the devil and all sorts of divers temptations.

For many years, until very recently, I have contended with the bitterness, disappointment, and hatred that have built up over these and many other related events. It has taken the power, love, mercy and forgiveness of God to deliver me from my own feelings. Hatred and bitterness can kill; they impact on the hater and the hated. If you are experiencing similar feelings due to related incidents, then the best medicine is to seek the love of God, to forgive others and yourself for harboring hatred and resentment of life's cruel blows. This is not an easy solution, but it is a lasting one. As we forgive, we are forgiven, and can continue on in great strength.

Alexis: My Life As "The Other Woman"

As a young girl, I was brought up to believe that adultery was wrong. I was adamantly opposed to adultery, and considered affairs something reserved for dirty women and movie stars. In spite of all my ideals, I stumbled into the real world, and eventually found myself in an adulterous relationship. About twenty years ago, my first husband and I were having a tumultuous marriage. I had carried all the hurt and anger into the marriage. I'm sure, looking back, that I had been hard to deal with. On the other hand, he was young, and wasn't ready for marriage either. We both had unresolved anger in our lives. Neither of us was committed to Jesus Christ, knew nothing about God's plans and instruction for marriage. I got pregnant on our honeymoon, one week after my dad died. I went from a cute 128 pounds to a crying, demanding, nearly 200 pound monster.

It was too much for my young husband. He found consolation in the arms of another girl. This is not an attempt to excuse them.

They were wrong. It was nobody's fault, or more accurately, it was the devil's fault. But pain, disappointment, anger, rejection, sudden shifts in responsibility all open the door for disillusioned lovers to seek new arms. My husband did.

For the next two years, my husband continued in affairs. One night, his girlfriend called while we were in bed. He was sleeping, I answered. He went to the phone. I was furious. I just couldn't stand adultery. To make a long story short, after many such incidents, including violent fights, I had enough. I never found out how he really felt. He said he wanted out. I filed for divorce, and returned home from the Army base where we were stationed, with my baby.

As soon as I got home, separated, hurt, lonely, disappointed and angry, I went out to a party with some old friends. Who did I discover but a young man I'd known from childhood. He was older than I was, but I'd had a secret "crush" on him all my life. He'd ignored me as a child, but he wasn't ignoring me any more. I told him I'd just gotten a divorce. He told me he and his wife were separated. The catch was, he and his wife had *discussed* divorce, they weren't getting along, but they were still married and living together. I allowed myself to believe what he said about her, never gave her a real thought. After all—I justified to myself—she didn't want him; their marriage was over.

It turns out that they did divorce later. He and I did not marry for many reasons. The real reason is that I never should have been involved with that dear lady's husband in the first place. I was wrong, wrong, wrong. I have never spoken to her, although I have wanted to apologize so many times. I really didn't want her husband so much as I just wanted a man of my own. The tragedy is, I tried to make her man into my own. It didn't work, and there was a lot of pain as a result. I tried to justify my behavior by telling myself that it hadn't been adultery; that I had never cheated while I was married, and that he wasn't really married.

12

This couple did remarry, and I rely on the blood of Jesus to cleanse me from my wrongdoing. I pray that they find Jesus and that their marriage will be strengthened.

Marva: Close Encounters With Other Women

I was very angry and immature during my first marriage. I didn't want to know the other women in my husband's life. I didn't want to know anything about them.

After my first divorce, I had an affair (dirty word, I just hate to admit that I did it). Although I only had one affair, I went on a rampage of "dating," or "romances." These words sounded much nicer than affairs, or even worse, "whoring around." With the exception of the one married man I dealt with, none of the men were married, and knowing little about the Lord Jesus Christ and the Word of God, I did just what I wanted to do. I was very pleased with myself, because being what some considered sexy and attractive, (I was a size 10/12, long hair, etc.) I had no trouble attracting men. I enjoyed seducing them, having them fall "in love"(?) with me, and then dumping them before they had a chance to hurt me. I couldn't handle rejection, yet always expecting it, I became a skilled rejecter. I was hurt, angry; I had experienced many losses in my life: my uncle's death, my dad's death, later my grandmom's death, and just before my second marriage, my sister's death. There was much pain and trauma moving from city to city, surviving house bombings, death threats, broken relationships.

During this time of my life, I didn't attend church regularly. I was working myself through college and supporting my child. My family didn't know a lot about what I was doing as far as my relationships were concerned. If they had, my father at least would have been devastated. I was on a seriously hell bent course. I had just come out of the second phase of an off-again on-again relationship with a married man. He was actually divorced at this time, although he had been married when we began dating. Our relationship wasn't working out. He became involved with other women while still dating me. I was angry because he insisted that if we married, he didn't want children. I wanted plenty of babies. It was another disaster.

As soon as we broke up (the married man and I), I went on the rebound, which is a very dangerous thing to do. A wounded woman or man, whose heart is bleeding from disappointment in love, is easy prey for the devil. Most often, casualties in the war of love wind up hurting others while getting hurt again themselves.

During this period, I experienced several romances, and an abortion. It took many years for me to get over the abortion. I spent hours wondering what kind of baby it was, a boy or a girl. I later began to feel very guilty. I covered up my many hurts by dating men. Women who have been hurt tend to seek solace in the arms of man after man.

I was no exception. I became tinvolved in a relationship with a man who I later became engaged to; only to find that he was bi-sexual and violent. I ran away from my hometown to escape this man, returned two years later to my separated/divorced man, only to break up with him for the final time. Right after the breakup, a dear

15

male friend of mine, married, and straight up with me, introduced me to the man who I would later marry.

I made another mistake. I considered this new man in my life my savior. I was miserable, and felt that my only redemption was a relationship with a man. When I became pregnant, he did the gentlemanly thing and married me. I worshiped him and hated him at the same time, because he reminded me of my daddy and all the other male role models in my life. He seemed to be the ideal image of a father and husband, yet, he liked to look at other women.

Needless to say, when he even looked at other women, I became livid. I felt that I was reliving my past, my mom's past and every other wronged woman's past. I had vowed that I would never let a man make a fool of me, and here I was fooled yet another time.

For years my second husband denied having affairs and told me that my insecurities were making me crazy. If some of the women hadn't come forth and admitted having affairs with him, I may have continued to believe that my past was merging with my present.

A very odd thing happened as I began to get to know the other women in my second husband's life. I had come to know Jesus Christ as my Lord and Savior just about the time these women began to admit to their affairs. As my marriage to my second husband began to break up, I found myself having candid conversations with at least three of the women he was intimately involved with. Two of these women asked me to forgive them for their relationships with my husband, and surprisingly, I did. I told each woman that I was more concerned with seeing them in Heaven than fighting with them here on earth. I remembered how I'd felt in their place, and had depended on God to forgive me. I found that by forgiving them, I helped them to forgive themselves, to admit to their wrongdoing in the situation, and to let go and get on with their lives.

It hasn't been so easy to forgive both of my husbands or my dad or all the other men I've looked to for answers. But I find that as I look more to God for the answers, and rely on the guidance of the Holy Spirit as I continue in life, the anger and bitterness is going away.

Today, I still desire a husband. I desire more to become the type of woman who can be a true wife. It is so much more important to get "me" right than to find the right man for me. I know the answer is not in finding, or more properly being found by a man, but to be complete in Jesus.

Candice: Why Women Go After Other Women's Men

After some serious soul searching, many painful memories, and another level of repenting, I was ready to consider the fact that women need men, and will do whatever is necessary to have a man in their lives.

Feminists and lesbians will resent this testimony, so I ask you in advance to forgive me.

In the Bible, the book of Genesis tells how God created Woman to be Man's helpmate. Due to Woman's part in Man's rebellion, God decreed that Man would live by the sweat of his brow, and Woman would cling to (need greatly) Man's attention, protection, love, and approval. I imagine that Man was pretty upset with Woman for her part in the rebellion and was not in much of a mood for love and approval. Over the hundreds of centuries, without the redemption of the curse from the shed blood of Jesus Christ, Woman continues to demand and crave Man's attentions. Woman craves love, Man more commonly craves sex.

Add to this a shortage of men, and you have women who pursue other women's men. The Bible describes situations where even godly men were allowed to honorably marry more than one woman at a time. Some men even today have as many as ten wives. These women have positions of honor. In our society, it is bigamy for a man to have more than one wife. We are also taught that it is a sin for a man to have more than one wife.

It is very puzzling to consider why even the New Testament tells bishops and deacons to be the husband of one wife, rather than to expressly say that all men should have only one wife. Jesus even used the parable of the ten brides waiting for the groom, and some not having enough oil and upon going out to by more oil for their lamps, some of the brides missed out on the marriage. For some reason, in many instances, God sanctioned unions of more than one wife. Maybe it was a shortage of men, and God's pity on the women and their need, or a desire to repopulate the earth, or a combination of both.

Today, especially in America and the Euro-Western culture, men in reality have multiple wives, who live under the guise of "girlfriend," and "mistress." These women are ostracized, and usually become brazen, heartless seductresses. In reality, they start out just like all women do. They want to be loved and needed. It is cruel and hypocritical to expect women not to have needs just because they do not have husbands. The need is not sin. The sin comes in when the women act out of their need and become involved in illicit relationships.

I am not suggesting or condoning polygamy for anyone who desires the excellent and holy life prescribed by Christ Jesus. It is just that women who have husbands would be better served to pray for women who do not. The sincere prayer of a married woman would go a lot further than suspicion and hatred.

It is condescending for a woman who has a husband, whose emotional, sexual and other needs are met, to look down upon

19

and judge single women who are struggling with desires to have these needs met. A woman's sexual and emotional desires do not diminish just because she finds herself unmarried. If she has been married, and these needs have been met, the woman is in for some very serious challenges and needs support and prayer to overcome temptation.

What single women need to be taught and what married women need to remember is that desire for a mate is ordained of God. God can and will fulfill these desires in the single woman, if she sincerely asks for His help. Some women are afraid to let go of these desires because they feel they will lose something. By trusting God, a woman cannot lose. God can preserve her pure and blameless until that mate comes forth.

A man or woman of spiritual fortitude would do best to choose the more excellent way of the Word and desire and cling to one mate. It is okay to desire a mate. It takes nothing away from a woman. We can still be intelligent, sensitive, and alive, and desire a mate, as long as our desire lines up with the will of God.

Living A Life Of Victory

The Bible, which is truly God's Word, tells us to flee fornication. The Word also tells us to shun childhood lusts. Many of the events described herein happened to other people. Yet, today, I too am often tempted. I take the Word of God literally, and flee situations that tempt me. Here are a few occasions where women have tested the Word mightily, and found it True.

Jackie: A Case Of Tight Pants

A friend once told me he didn't believe I've ever seen an ugly man. In other words, I find something good in everybody. This being the case, there are still some features about men that are especially trying for me. I personally, in the flesh, am attracted to firm, strong legs in a man. Many times, I have to resist the devil when I am in the presence of men with nice legs. Don't get me wrong, I am saved, sanctified and filled with the Holy Ghost. I don't want to fornicate or commit adultery, but legs still give me a problem.

During a recent period of my life, I was in a professional environment with a certain man. Sometimes, he would wear pants that fit him quite well. It was distracting to me. This was my problem, not his. He, beyond a professional respect, was not involved with me in any way. But, I had a problem. I was attracted to his legs, and to his position of power.

I believe this often happens to women. They become attracted to men in positions of power and authority, and then a natural attraction sets in. If the woman or the man acts on this attraction, they are in trouble!

In this case, I did not act upon the attraction. Thank God I didn't. I would have received a severe reprimand from the man, I am sure.

Ladies, this is very important. If you find yourselves in trouble, pray, repent, flee! God will help you resist the devil. The Holy Spirit is ready and willing to lead you out of trouble. The ministering angels will fight for you. Turn to God, not the lusts of the flesh.

Praise God, I didn't act on my flesh. Looking back, I wish I had prayed the thing through.

Instead, I did a very ignorant thing; I went to the man's wife and told her I had a problem with his pants. Thank goodness the man and the woman were both much more mature than I was. They never mentioned the matter again. However, the man did stop wearing those pants, which was a relief. Other ladies had remarked about the pants in the same professional setting. They just had more tact and maturity at that time, than I had. They prayed rather than blabbed about it.

I later developed a stronger professional relationship with the man and his wife. I have learned to regard them and people like them with greater respect, and to deal with the problems of my flesh in prayer, rather than with my mouth.

Cheryl: The Beautiful Egyptian Queen

Very recently, I have been confronted with a very challenging situation. In my working/professional environment, I am in constant contact with attractive men, be they colleagues or even clients. Now, I am saved, not dead. I am aware of attractive men. They often stop and give me compliments, which I try to graciously acknowledge and keep moving.

On a particular day, one colleague, whom I had noticed before, and had often responded to in passing greetings, met me as I was walking up the walkway. He is very tall, well built, and speaks with an accent. This day he spoke with a broad smile, "You look like a beautiful Egyptian princess." I was walking with someone, and actually became flustered knowing that I thought this man attractive. I answered, "Thank you," and started walking faster. The man turned, his voice following me as I was making a fast retreat. "I really mean it. You look like a beautiful Egyptian queen."

I rushed inside to my colleague who, years before, had led me to Christ, explained to her what had happened, and pleaded, "Pray. I like him. The man probably is married, with ten wives."

With the wisdom of God, she smiled and said, "It's up to you. You know the Word."

She was right. I know the Word. That's why at first, I would take off running every time I would see this man. It doesn't pay to flirt with temptation.

Since that time, this man and I have developed a sincere friendship and have talked about Jesus and many other topics. I managed to overcome my flesh and relate to him without running.

If you see a woman running for the hills, don't laugh, pray. She probably needs direction and protection. Help her to find that place where she can shout: The victory is mine!

Hannah: A Handmaiden's Testimony

Author's note: The woman who gives this testimony is very special. There are not many women who are more beautiful and humble, inside and out. She has a beautiful spirit, and is used wonderfully by God to bring joy and hope to everyone she comes in contact with.

When I read some of the other women's testimonies, I knew that I had a message to share. I am sure that many women who have suffered as I have can benefit from the wonderful truth I have found.

When I was three months old, I was separated from my mother and nine brothers and sisters because my mother had experienced an affair of which I was the result. She decided not to abort me, so I was born. My father was married to another woman. My mother's husband hated me and tried to kill me. So at the age of three months, I was given to the insurance lady, who adopted me. My adopted family loved me in their own way, but they never drew me close to them. I didn't look like anybody in my new family, and always felt like "the ugly duckling."

When I was twelve, my adopted mother told me the true circumstances of my life. I was shattered, devastated. Somehow, I died right then. All emotional development ceased. I could feel nothing but rage, anger, hurt and pain. Because I did not like to feel these negative emotions, I elected to not feel at all. Thus began several years of wild living: sex, alcohol, and suicide attempts.

I got pregnant and married when I was twenty. Somehow, (and not just somehow, but rather by the grace of God), I had survived my teen years. My first husband was very violent, and I left him eight months after we were married. He, like all the other men before him, did not measure up to the "daddy" I was searching for ever since I had been deprived of my own.

Within months, I met my second husband, and married him. I was still hurt, angry, bitter at my life circumstances. I would curse anyone who crossed my path, because I felt the world owed me something. My second husband was the exception. He became the "daddy" I never had. He taught me how to cook, to think, and to a certain extent to feel. He was really my god. I had no way of knowing how ugly all of this was to the real, true God.

My life had been ugly, and as a result I was ugly, and I thought I had a right to be. I had no way of knowing that Jesus had paid the price of my pain, and was ready to deliver me, make something beautiful of my life.

In a miserable way, I was content with my co-dependent life. My husband was my god; I was his responsibility. We fulfilled each other's needs.

Then, I met Jesus. Through Jesus, I came to know God the Father, and to be filled with the Holy Spirit. I began to see through new eyes. I began to understand the hurt of the mother who had given me away. I began to consider that I might need to answer the letters she'd been writing. I began to understand the pain and hurt of the father I'd never known and lost to death. My father's wife was in pain too, and wanted to meet me. I wasn't ready to meet her, but I understood her pain. I understood the sacrifice of my adopted mother, and because of the adoption of the family of man through the blood of Jesus Christ, adoption took on a new meaning for me.

I began to understand forgiveness, the need to forgive as well as be forgiven. I even began to understand the rage and confusion of my second husband, who felt he was losing me to someone, even though that someone was Jesus.

During the last few years, prayer has led many of my husband's family to Christ. It is my great desire and belief that he too will come into the fullness of Christ, and together we will know the joy of serving the Lord.

Do not weep or feel sorry for me. I have discovered who my real enemy is. Man, woman nor child has ever hurt me. My enemy has always been the devil. Since I found Jesus, I have gained victory over my enemy. Somewhere, in the process of my life, I have gained something very beautiful. I have become very close to Jesus. Through all of these experiences, I have gained a heart of compassion for those who are hurting. As I have learned to forgive all the injuries in my life, Jesus has ministered a wonderful healing balm to all my wounds. Sometimes, we can only experience the joy and wonder of God's love after we lose ourselves and all that we consider dear. This happened to me, and the love and grace and mercy I have found to replace all that I believed had been taken away is something words cannot express.

I say to women who have been hurt, there is an answer. Cast your cares upon Him (Jesus) and He will sustain you. He will transform pain to joy.

Cassandra: A Pure Woman

Author's note: When I met this woman, I was amazed. Jesus once spoke of a man in whom there was no guile. I have found no guile in Cassandra. I've not heard her use profanity, nor speak ill of anyone. She is a true example of purity and virtue.

I was married to one man for many years. I have never known (had sex with) another man. My husband and I were very happy. We had three children, and our family has always been my life. I am now a widow in my early forties.

Since my husband is gone, after two years, I am almost ready to let another man know my heart. I have recently met a man who approaches me gently and correctly.

It was several weeks before I gave him my phone number. We have been seeing each other for three months. I do not have his phone number. I have never cooked for him. I allow him to hold my hand. He says that my skin is soft.

I have continued to tell him that I am not concerned about his personal life and activities beyond our relationship. One day, he called me by another lady's name. I told him that I was offend-ed because my name is beautiful, and I couldn't understand why he would mistake me for someone else. I am not naive, I am sure he is seeing someone else. But it is not my desire to question nor challenge him. The Bible says "he who finds a wife, finds a good thing." I am not looking for a man, nor a husband; he found me. It is his responsibility to know what he wants.

Adrianne: Religion is not the answer.

When I see women so involved in causes and movements, I remember the days when I was into "Black Awareness," "Transcendental Meditation," "Mother Earth," Women's Lib," and many of the movements that came in during the 1960's. I wore the ankh (an Egyptian cross representing life), burned incense, chanted as part of deep meditation in the Buddhist faith, wore African and Middle-Eastern garments, sought truth in the Suni-Muslim, Hebrew-Islamic Muslim, Black Hebrew, Ausar-Auset and New Age religions. In short, I grabbed hold to any thing and any body who appeared to represent truth. My life was one big religious experience.

I followed whatever man I happened to be involved with at the time down the primrose path of whatever religion he was into. I was seeking love, affection, and truth, but I really didn't know what truth was. There was something enchanting about the combination of religion/philosophy, wine, (illicit) sex, and pulsating music. I was looking for what I called my inner self, some deep truth.

For some reason, I didn't see the correlation between the various religions. And yet, looking back, they were similar. Certain dress codes, special requirements and rituals, exclusive of everyone who didn't share the same view, all religion is a system of laws and requirements. All religion promises truth, but the truth is, religion doesn't deliver.

The Bible says that we should know the truth, and the truth will set us free. Jesus said knock and it shall be opened unto you. I truly believe that most people who take part in the types of religions I have mentioned here, and in fact any types of religions, are seeking truth. The only thing is, they find the real truth too simple or too complicated (depending on their perspectives) to take hold of. The Lord Jesus Christ said (and continues to say since He is eternal), "I am the way, the truth and the life. No man comes to the Father except he (or she) come by me." Since God created Man, male and female created He them (Genesis 1), then Man male and Man female must come to the realization that Jesus is who He says He is.

There is nothing new about any religious sect. All religion is founded on man's effort to know and reach God or whatever represents God to them, be it idol gods or inner self, or any source outside oneself. In Ecclesiastes, King Solomon puts it aptly: "There is no new thing under the sun."

The New World Order, or the New Age Movement as it is often called, is not new at all. Actually it can be considered the daddy of religion. This is a religion that was established to lead people to believe that they can become part of God's family without accepting His Son Jesus Christ, who is the only way, the truth and the life. The presentation of this movement is subtle, and suggests that there is a family of man, embraced by all religions, and that God is going to accept everybody into Heaven whether they believe in the resurrected Jesus Christ or not. This movement will usher in the anti-christ, will introduce the mark of the beast on the forehead and right hand, probably with computer chips in the head or the right wrist. This movement teaches that God is too loving and good to allow people to go to hell. This is not true. God is good and loving, that is why He sent His Son Jesus. If people do not receive Him, they will go to hell. The black man has no place in the New World Order. Actually, the New World Order isn't new after all. The doctrine of the New World Order dates back to the time of Nimrod, and many of the Eastern religions have foundational precepts that are similar to those found in the New World Order.

For the woman who is looking for the man of her dreams, the man's belief system must, for her, be a priority. A man must have his foundations firmly established in the truth of the Bible, and the Lordship of Jesus the Christ. A woman should desire a man who knows who he is in Jesus, who knows his purpose and who is willing to answer the call of God on his life.

You may wonder, *What are the advantages of accepting this call?* Life in Christ Jesus gives many great advantages:
1. Eternal life, which includes a new body, a royal commission, a permanent fellowship with God.
2. Protection from harm under the blood covenant of Christ Jesus.
3. Power by the infilling of the Holy Spirit.
4. Prosperity, divine health, abundant blessings of God.

Many Muslim and Hebrew religions emphasize the covenant of Abraham. The Bible teaches that it is very special to be Abraham's natural seed. Yet God provides a better covenant through the shed blood of Jesus Christ. While Abraham's covenant (embraced by many eastern religions) provides us with blessings when we obey God (see Deuteronomy 28) the covenant of the shed blood of Jesus Christ provides us with eternal life.

33

Consider John 3:16: *For God so loved the world, that He gave His only Begotten Son, that you can believe on Him, and have everlasting life.* Experience the benefits of both covenants. Accept Jesus today, and live.

Pray this prayer now, with all of your heart, mean it when you pray it. As you believe, you will receive.

Dear Heavenly Father, in the name of Jesus, I come. I believe that your only begotten son came in the flesh, went to Calvary, and died on the cross for me. On the third day, He was raised from the dead, that I might be set right with God. Jesus, come now into my heart, into my life. Take away the old, the guilt and condemnation of the past. Give me your life, your peace, your joy, your strength, your faith, and your love. I believe I receive salvation now. I believe I receive the Lord Jesus as my Savior. I give you my word, today, now, I'll live for you and serve you all the days of my life. Thank you Father, in Jesus' name, for hearing my prayers. Thank you Jesus, for being my Savior and Lord. Hallelujah! I'm saved! Now fill me with your mighty Holy Spirit. Thank you Lord Jesus, my healer, my friend. I'm saved, filled, redeemed from the curse of sin. Amen.

Odessa: God Speaks To A Beloved

The origin of this conversation with God is unknown. It continues to circulate around the world. It came to my hands by Odessa, a beloved sister in Christ.

Everybody longs to give themselves completely to someone, to have a deep soul relationship with another so as to be loved thoroughly and exclusively. But, God, to the Christian said: "No, not until you are satisfied, fulfilled, and content with being loved by Me; with giving yourself totally and unreservedly to Me, to having an intensely personal and unique relationship with Me, alone.

"Only in Me is your satisfaction to be found. Will you be capable of the perfect human relationship that I have planned for you? You will never be united with another until you are united with Me.

"Exclusive of any one or anything else, exclusive of any other desire or longing, I want you to stop planning, stop wishing, and follow Me and I will give you the most thrilling plan existing. One that you cannot imagine; I want you to have the best. Please allow me to bring it to you.

"You just wait, that's all. Don't be anxious; don't worry. Don't look around at others and the things they have, or that I've given them. Don't look at the things you think you want. You just keep looking off and away up to me, or you'll miss what I want to show you. When you're ready, I'll surprise you with a love far more wonderful than you could ever imagine. You must wait until the one I have for you is ready, (I am working even at this moment to have you both ready at the same time). Until you are both satisfied exclusively with me and the life I've prepared for you, you won't be able to experience the love that exemplifies your relationship with me. You will enjoy materially and concretely the everlasting union and love that I offer you. Believe It And Be Satisfied!"

Odessa speaks: As I read this testimony, I was reminded of something I had recently gone through. After having been married, having raised children, having been hurt so many times, I had become very bitter. Once I was in the house when a man broke in and raped my mother, and tried to rape me before running away, as if chased by some mysterious force. I had been taken from my mother who couldn't care for us, and separated from my brothers and sisters because I was the only dark skinned one of the brood. My aunts wanted the other children because they were "pretty." I was sent to live with my grandmother, and forbidden to tell my younger siblings that I was their sister. They were adopted and became part of a family but I was not welcomed.

Later, I became pregnant. The baby's father promised to marry me, and didn't, and went away to Viet Nam. I had an abortion. I became even more bitter. In my early twenties, I married a celebrity whom I wooed away from his wife, only to find myself beaten and abused and exposed to incredible perversions during this marriage.

Many years and many relationships later, as the pain subsided, I had learned to be content. Raising my teenagers alone, I came to a relationship with Christ, and convinced myself that I would never need another man. I'm sure I had a secret longing, but I was so afraid of the hurt and pain that came hand in hand with relationships. At least that was the way I viewed life with men, pain and pleasure. And the pleasure just wasn't worth the pain anymore.

And then—Bang! I met this man who turned my whole world upside down. Here I was, a grandmother, a seasoned woman, and my heart would pound every time I came into his presence. I couldn't handle it. I was thinking about him all the time. And we didn't even have a relationship. He was younger and wanted marriage and children, something that was behind me. And yet, he spoke kindly to me. Told me that I was beautiful, and that sort of thing. We could talk. He made me feel alive.

I found myself talking about him to everyone, making an absolute fool of myself. I began to long for this man more than for my precious Lord Jesus. And then, one day as I was driving along, it hit me. The way I was feeling about this man is the way I needed to feel about God. I started weeping. "God," I said, "I can live without him. I can live without everything but you. I love you! Don't be jealous. I love you!" I broke into singing "How Great Thou Art," as the tears flooded. I later admitted to God that I wanted to have a man who loves God as much if not more than I do, so that together we can love God.

As I reflected upon my condition, this testimony from the unknown writer began to be real to me. I just know that God has something special for me. If not the heart throb in this passage, then someone just for me, planned and designed by my Father. Glory!

Kenya: If You Want It To Work, Work At It

Author's note: Kenya is a delightful person to know, respected by her peers and associates. She is a successful career woman, model housewife, catalogue shopper, and bargain hunter. You can often find people gathered at her desk for advice, or just to share a moment of her company.

I never had much interest in getting married. I had seen my parents' marriage destroy my mother's life and my father's. I witnessed the negative impact the fighting had on my sisters, my brothers and me. I watched my parents use us as weapons against each other. Later, I watched my sisters divorce and sensed the pain it left on their children. I held on to this conviction until my late 30's when something unforeseeable happened—a long time friendship developed into a very strong love—and this person had custody of his two year old child. I found myself in conflict with a twenty-five year conviction against marriage.

There were other problems—hostile in-laws, an unpredictable ex-wife, and enormous financial problems left over from the previous marriage, not to mention a child entering the "terrible twos." There were more reasons not to marry than there were to marry, but I loved him and so I prayed long and hard. The answer came to me clear—this was the man the Lord had sent and this was the child from my lost childhood. My trust could not lie in my own understanding. It had to rest wholly and without question in the Lord's decision. So despite my quiet fears—we married.

The first two years of my marriage were plagued with all the painful adjustments two people could face. In-laws who believed that my husband's loyalty belonged first to them, disagreements in child rearing, finances completely out of control and a husband who retreats in the face of conflict. Many times I questioned my own decision. I felt no love and support from my husband those first two years of marriage. But I continued to pray. I continued to recall in my own mind the love we felt for each other for so many years before. I continued to trust that the Lord had mapped the way through this period and soon his plan would be revealed.

Finally the day came. The bills were paid, fights with the in-laws had subsided, our child was happy and entering school, we were moving into our own house—the door was open for the love to return. And then it happened—a discussion led to an argument and the argument led to words being spoken—words of condemnation I had heard many times from my in-laws, but never thought I would hear from the man I loved. That night I sat on my new porch and angrily challenged God—why had he taken me this far just to give me something I could have found on any street corner. "I kept my promise," I said. "Should it now be obvious to me that You did not intend to keep Yours?" I often think of the words I spoke that night and I shudder, for the years that followed brought me more happiness than I ever thought to ask for.

With God's love and direction, we forgave each other for the angry words and actions. The man the Lord had given to me showered me with more love than I knew I could contain. The child that is now my child—the child that was so like the me of years ago, can laugh, as I never could laugh, can do childish things, can dream, and because of her enormous love for me, I can now put the sad and lonely child inside me to rest. Thank You Father!

Louise: A Tribute To A Friend

Brenda and I have been friends for many years. As young women, we spent a lot of time together. We were both students, although Brenda was pursuing her masters degree and I was working towards my bachelors. I secretly wanted to be just like her. I admired her, and yet I was jealous of her. I never admitted this to Brenda, but somehow, I believe she knew.

We were both what you might consider attractive. She is tall and statuesque; I am just above average height with heavy legs. I usually wore my hair long, she wore shorter styles. While we have both always been intelligent, she was scholarly. I was more artistic, reactionary. I believe a scholarly nature would have served me better, but you don't have a choice.

When we met, we'd both been married and divorced, and had decided to continue with our pursuit of various goals. I had no idea what I wanted to be or to do. Brenda, on the other hand, had a road map. As we continued on, she met her second husband, a quiet, handsome man who had no greater aspiration than to love and cherish her. He was not motivated to achieve great intellectual heights, but was happy to have a wife who was now pursuing her doctorate.

Soon after Brenda finished her doctoral program, which she completed in record time, their marriage ended, pretty much by mutual agreement. I didn't understand why she wasn't content to just go on with things the way they were, but it wasn't my life.

About two years after her divorce, Brenda married again. This time she married a professional man, and soon after, they moved away. By then she had published two books, and was to receive a handsome appointment at a highly respected institution. Her reputation had preceded her. As a scholar, she was superb. She was, and still is today, a beautiful, intelligent, accomplished woman.

When Brenda went away we stayed in touch, but didn't write or call often. I was very pleased to have people know that she was my friend, because of her fine reputation. I still wasn't able to admit fully that I was jealous of her. I secretly found fault with her, although she was really a special and beautiful person, and friend.

As time went by, Brenda and her third husband had a baby. This was accomplished with the same aplomb with which Brenda accomplishes everything in life. The baby, like Brenda, was beautiful and intelligent. Even though, by this time, I had many accomplishments under my belt—career, husband, children, publications, I still felt that I did not measure up to Brenda.

The thing that hurts the most has always been my treachery in light of Brenda's attitude. She is so sincere and so loving and supportive. She always rejoices at my victories, and supports me in my pain. I tended to give lip service to her accomplishments, although I could sympathize with her pain. Even though I felt for her during her hard times, I also felt glad that something was going wrong in her all too perfect life.

Now, Brenda and I are both divorced again. Somehow, even hard knocks haven't affected her in an extremely adverse way. She just goes on to bigger and better things. Now that I have admitted how I've felt about her, I believe that I too can move on to something greater.

For those of you who wonder what this testimony has to do with the theme of this book, consider this. I never went after any of Brenda's men, although I think her second husband was precious. I didn't want Brenda's man; I wanted her whole life. The same jealousies and insecurities that deceive women into going after other women's men had me coveting my friend's life. I wanted to look like her, think like her, be like her, but I didn't want to pay the price of discipline and sacrifice. I wanted what she had, and therefore didn't learn to appreciate her for what she is.

This testimony is for all the men and women who are not realizing their potential because they are coveting someone else's dreams. Let go of what they have, and find out who you are.

Brie: All Monsters Are Not In The Movies

As Alveda and I sat talking, she admitted that although she is very daring and open, she was hesitant to print this segment. We were sharing various incidents that we know of, really true situations. She reluctantly decided to print this, even if some of it sounds strange and unbelievable, because these things all really happened.

This particular thing happened to me. I was dating a man, and he did all of the cooking. We dated for many months, and I began to lose sight of myself. It was like he had control of me, mentally and physically. It was like I had no real mind of my own. I became weak and listless, my blood count was low. I didn't want to make decisions on my own, I looked to him to do everything for me. I worked, but a lot of my vitality was gone.

When I went to the doctor, he discovered I had a very low blood count. It became apparent that I was losing a lot of blood during intimate activity. It all began to add up. My boyfriend was slipping drugs into my food, and controlling my mind and body by other creative ways against my knowledge, and was actually ingesting my blood.

We have all read or seen dracula stories. This man didn't grow long fangs and bite my neck, but he was draining my life away. Somehow, and today I believe it was by the grace of God, I came to my senses and ran away from this man. Today, I know the Lord, and rely on the Word of God to protect me from all evil. Psalms 91 is a favorite of mine. When bad dreams or memory recall would overtake me, I remember that "no harm" can come near my dwelling.

God's angels have charge over me, to protect me from the terrors of night and the dangers of the daytime. This is something that people need to know. God is really bigger than the devil. Jesus has all power over every evil. He sent the Greater One (The Holy Spirit) to live in us to overcome fear and death and danger. But we have to know God in order to overcome.

Some people think that if you don't believe in witchcraft, black magic or the occult, then it can't hurt you. There are a lot of dead people who believed that. What makes these evil works not hurt you is the power of God. The tragedy is, many times, people of darkness study harder than Christians. They get to know their dark arts better than we know the Bible. But when we do God's Word, we always come out the victors. Let me tell you about a wise warrior woman who understands the power of God.

This particular woman married a successful business man. She was a business woman herself. They proceeded to have and raise a family, to participate in church and social and community activities. As time went on, the man wanted to control his wife. She was changing. She wanted to read the Bible all the time. She would go away from their home church and visit crusades when they came to town. She started bringing home books about healings, tongues, miracles and other materials that were unfamiliar and unlike the traditional doctrine they had accepted for years. The man felt his control over their home slipping.

As the wife grew more and more in the things she was learning, things started to happen in the house. She would find odd little packages hidden around the house in strange places, like in the soles of her shoes, far under unused cabinets. The packages would have her hair and other personal objects in them. Sometimes, she would get sick for days, or depressed, and no doctor could tell her what was wrong. The worse things became, the more she sought after things of God.

She began to learn that reading the Bible kept her from losing her mind, and from falling victim to the clutches of the strange illnesses that tried to overtake her.

As time went on, as her children grew older, her husband's tactics grew more and more deliberate. If he could not control her, he would make sure that she suffered. He began to let her know about other women who constantly pursued him. He would harass her, deprive her of sleep, badger her.

They moved into separate bedrooms. He began to paint a picture to the public of her as the villain. In truth, he was the villain. But the Word of God won out. She had called upon the name of the Lord and was saved, redeemed from darkness and evil. No weapon formed against her would prosper.

After their children grew older, they divorced. She has fought a hard battle against bitterness, and by the grace of God, she has won. Today, she is beautiful and wise, and is able to counsel men and women who are under satanic, occult attack. Her weapons are not carnal, but are mighty to the tearing down of strongholds. Her armor is the armor of Ephesians 6.

Witchcraft is real, but the Power of God is more real. If you are involved in witchcraft, as the victim or the user, get out. God does not honor one human's control over another, for any reason.

The only legitimate way to get a mate is by the way proposed in God's Word. "Delight yourself in the Lord, and He will give you the desires of your heart." We must not use supernatural forces to get what we want according to our own desires. We must turn to the supernatural God, and expect Him to guide us into truth and happiness.

Regina: My Choice Over God's

Author's note: Regina is precious and brilliant. She has been told that God wants to use her in a mighty way, as a hammer for justice. She has fought to overcome the idolatry of intellect which is common to men and women of great natural intelligence and gifts. As a yielded vessel of God, she is very dangerous to the devil.

As a young woman, I had great expectations. I wanted to become a professional in an area that was greatly respected, and mostly reserved for men. I also had ideals of love, marriage, and family. I didn't know Jesus as my Lord, but I had experienced a sense of God all my life. Even as a little girl, I would talk to God. Early in my life, God spoke to me and told me what career path to follow. Even though everyone tried to discourage me from this maverick path, I would not be deterred.

I always had a strong will, and wanted to have my way. As a child, my mother would tell me, "Don't touch the stove; it's hot." I was determined to touch it anyway, and would. I wanted to do what I wanted to do. This strong-willed spirit was born in me, and although my parents were strict on me, I nevertheless grew into adulthood expecting to have my way; determined not to listen to the voice of authority.

As I grew into adulthood, I became convinced that my way was the best way in everything. This worsened after I had achieved one of life's goals and became one of the few women in a highly respected profession. By that time, I wouldn't listen to anyone else or even God for that matter. When people would try to steer me in the right direction, I would say, "God didn't tell me that. I have to hear Him." As a result, I made many costly mistakes in my life. My stubbornness affected my health, my finances, and my love life.

My first costly mistake occurred during my early adulthood. I fell in love with the man who should have been my husband; the man whom God had picked for me. But, I couldn't believe God to pave the way. When we met, we were both well into preparing for our careers, and he had great expectations of a future political career. I, on the other hand, had a child from another relationship, and I couldn't envision myself as the wife of a prominent political figure. This was years ago, and at that time, it was socially frowned upon to have a child out of wedlock. My doubts about our relationship were reinforced by his parents, who thought that my past would be harmful to his future career. Although he also loved me very much, he struggled with the choice of love or parental acceptance.

Propelled by fear, anxiety and impatience, I refused to wait for him to choose. Fear gripped me that a marriage would not work between us. I was anxious to remove the stigma of being an unwed mother. And, I was impatient, wanting to have a husband of my own. This man promised to marry me, but kept putting it off. I didn't know God well enough, and hadn't accepted Jesus as my Lord, so I had nothing to fall back on. I knew this man and we loved each other, but when he began to hedge, I wavered in God's word to me. I grew hurt and angry. I felt betrayed, and in a fit of impatience and despair, I married another man.

This other man was not God's choice for me. I willfully did what I wanted to do because I was hurt. As a result, my husband never felt that I really loved him. I did love him, but not in the way he deserved to be loved. As a result, he felt betrayed, became abusive and began to have affairs outside of our marriage.

My life was a mess. I couldn't see how my true feelings caused my husband's actions. I felt betrayed by my husband, but I still loved the man of my youth. My marriage ended in divorce. To make matters worse, I couldn't go back to the man I truly loved, for he was hurt and angry and felt betrayed by me too. He told me that he always planned and desired to marry me, and that if I had waited, rather than rushing off to marry my husband, he would have worked things out and married me.

Now, many years later, my former husband, my life's love, and I are all unmarried. My former husband remarried and has divorced again. The man from my youth married shortly after I married, but the marriage was very brief. He is now divorced. He never had the children he so desperately wanted to have with me. Painfully and strangely, both men seem to love and hate me at the same time.

I, myself, feel only regret: regret for the hurt I have caused two beautiful men; regret for the devastating effect the abusive marriage and subsequent divorce had upon my precious children; and regret for the life that I forfeited out of my own stubborn willfulness.

Even though I confessed Christ as my savior many years ago, I, at first, wouldn't live the life of a submitted Christian. I wanted to do things my way. Even after many knocks and falls, I'd use my own strength to get up, and go on my stubborn way. I was determined to deal with the pain and hurt on my own. I tried to heal the wounds I had inflicted on these two men and my children. However, the more I tried, the worse the relationships became. My son turned bitter against me, and he still holds me responsible for the divorce and his separation from his father.

I now realize that only God can heal. He says, in His Word, "I am the Lord thy God Who healeth thee." God is not a man that He should lie. He expects us to believe His word for He says, without faith it is impossible to please Him. He assures us that He hastens to perform His Word; that His Word shall not return to Him void but that It shall accomplish that for which It is sent.

My situation would seem hopeless, but for God's Word. God wants us to hear His voice and turn away from hopelessness and despair. "Come to Me, all you who labor and are heavy laden, and I will give you rest. Take My yoke upon you and learn from Me, for I am gentle and lowly in heart, and you will find rest for your souls. For My yoke is easy and My burden is light." Matthew 11:28-30.

God promises us the best. He says that he would not withhold any good thing from us. Though my lesson has been hard, I am persuaded in the promises of God. You need not fall into great pain and suffering, as I did, if you will only trust in and rely upon God in finding a mate. We must all learn to make Jesus Christ Lord, and only move in the things He ordains. He is the Truth, Way and Life. His way is sure and His blessings add no sorrow. Through Jesus Christ I have great faith that I will surely come into the blessings that He has for me. If you will be led by His Spirit and yield your will to Him, You will also surely come into the blessings that He has for you. And, we have this assurance in Him: His blessings will be greater than we can ever think or ask.

T'ana: Redeemed From
The Curse

Many years ago, when I had my first baby, I astounded people. When I went into labor, it was no big deal. I decided to wash my hair, go to the store, bake a cake and do some cleaning. When a contraction would come, I would simply say, "Excuse me a moment," and take a deep breath and then go on with whatever I was doing. The baby was born one hour after I arrived at the hospital.

This was all years before the Lamaze Method of Childbirth became all the rage. I went on to have several more children. With all of my children, my labor pains were mild, nominal, and in many instances, I didn't feel them at all. With two exceptions, all of my babies were born an hour after I arrived at the hospital. I spent only one night in a hospital labor room, and that's because I was older, and wanted to see what it was all about, this "laying in." It was no fun at all.

I am relating this because I believe that's what God desires for all women. I really believe that God wants women to be free from every curse of sin and death. That is why God sent Jesus Christ into the world, to redeem Man (and Woman) from the curse that came because of Adam's and Eve's sin. Labor pains are a curse.

In the Bible, in the book of Genesis, chapter 3, after Adam and Eve had eaten of the forbidden fruit, God cursed them. Adam was cursed with hard work and grief and the prospect of death. At the fall, Adam and Eve suffered immediate spiritual death (they were cut off from God) and the prospect of physical death, where they had once expected to live forever. They no longer had the joys of a cooperative planet. The earth was cursed, where once it had been a blessing for Adam's sake.

Eve's curse was almost a double indemnity. She received the curse of Adam, and also a curse that would lead to much pain and sorrow. She would conceive children in pain, she would birth them in pain, she would live to see some of her children die, and be forced into exile from their family. Eve was also cursed with having to turn her desire away from God to her husband, and he would rule over her.

Eve no longer had the loving, happy companion of the Garden. She was faced with constantly longing and desiring the companionship of a man who no longer had time for her. Adam was now forced to conquer a hostile earth. The animals had become ferocious, food had to be cultivated, the elements had to be dealt with. The constant temperature of Eden was no longer available to Adam, so he had to worry about feeding, clothing, and protecting his family.

So, man and woman were cursed. For generations, women have lived under "the curse." We have longed for love and been hurt and rejected. We have been plagued with female problems. We have pursued men who were not right for us, because of the unfortunate desire for man that came with "the curse."

This is why so many women fall into fornication and adultery. They want love, they desire a man at all costs. The good news is that Jesus came to destroy the works of the devil, to set the captives free. Women do not have to be bound to emotional imbalance, hormonal imbalance, and physical problems. Once we accept Jesus, we are really free from the curse.

This does not mean that we are released from certain female functions, like childbearing, nursing babies, menstruation and the like. But we do not have to suffer as so many women do. We can fulfill all of God's plans for woman, and still live free from the curse. The curse is the discomfort; discomfort of childbearing; discomfort of menopause; discomfort of longings and heartache; discomfort of female diseases. We can, through the Word of God, be free from the curse.

When I began to really understand the price Jesus had paid for me (Isaiah 53:5); how he was wounded for my past acts of fornication, drinking; how he was bruised for my labor pains, my hot flashes; how surely he has long ago and forever borne the sorrow of my abortions and broken relationships; and how with and by His precious stripes, I am healed, set free and delivered, I just wanted to shout, dance, and rejoice.

Dear, dear, ladies, get a hold of this truth. You can live free from the curse. Jesus paid the price for you. You don't have to sleep around with men anymore. You don't have to curse, and flirt, and drink and do drugs, and go to bed and wake up feeling dirty the next morning. Jesus paid it all. He has delivered a cashier's check to you. All you have to do is take it to the bank and cash it. Start living the life of freedom that God wants for you. It is real, and it is your's for the asking. Wake up and live. Be free!

Jeannie: A Love Like Ours

Jason and I were married almost half a century ago. The country was in flux, the world was very romantic, the word chaos was still new enough to those in my social circle as to be exciting rather than provoking panic.

After rising from modest beginnings to live a life of luxurious globe trotting, I was just jaded enough to desire something less demanding than the life I had been living. My profession was interior design. I had an eye for fine art, and could decorate with a passion. Many would have considered me beautiful. I considered myself exotic instead, with large ears, even larger eyes, and everything else petite in contrast. I had had lovers, but had never really loved, when gentle, artistic, and yet strong and exciting Jason entered my life.

It was more like a storybook romance than anything, I guess. We met at a party and then didn't see each other again for months. Our next meeting was just as incidental as the first. He was a world famous architect, designer of playgrounds for the rich and famous. Houses, estates, professional buildings, these were

Jason's world. I was a pampered woman of the world, admired and desired by many, yet loved by no one.

After we were married, we moved about in a world of luxury and fame. He designed homes for stars like Elizabeth Taylor and the like. His designs appeared in famous magazines. He built our dream home. He began on the project of a lifetime. We were developing a valley resplendent with homes, recreation facilities, shopping and moderate commercial outlets. It was to be beautiful and yet functional.

At the very height of Jason's career, he found Jesus. His whole life changed. He came alive in a way that was so different from his normal zest for life. His favorite expression to our friends who challenged his new found faith was, "Either Jesus is who he says He is, or He's the world's greatest liar or lunatic. I've tried Him, I've challenged Him. He is real."

I didn't accept Christ at first. Jason, in his love and regard for me, was infinitely patient. He sent me to India to study with the Maharishi. He allowed my pursuit into the middle eastern religions, while praying for me all along. As a result, right in the middle of a meditation session, I began to remember some of Jason's beliefs. I began to question the Maharishi. There were questions he couldn't answer. The Bible and other history books were too accurate. Jesus was not just a prophet, or a good man who went about doing good. Jesus was and is the son of God!

I returned home with a burning desire to know Christ. Jason welcomed me with open arms. We continued on together in a life of love and witness, until he was attacked by a long term illness, and finally went to be with the Lord. I was hurt and angry with God for allowing Jason to die. I was depressed and even suicidal for many days. Then the Lord rescued me. I have continued on with the knowledge that I will be reunited with Jason, in heaven, and am allowing God to use me until the time comes.

I really don't desire another marriage. The love that I shared with Jason was once in a lifetime. Only the love of Christ could ever surpass our love. And in Christ, nothing is lost, only completed.

The Lady: A Virtuous Woman, Who Can Find?

Author's note: This lady is a beautiful example of what we as women should seek to be. She is lovely and gracious inside and out.

Many years ago, I married my childhood sweetheart. In the early years, our marriage was a great challenge. We did not know the Lord. My husband always says this: "My daddy was a deacon, my mama sang on the choir, and I sat on the back row, on my way to hell." He had little knowledge of the Lordship of Jesus Christ. He remembers seeing a little old lady running up and down the aisle of the church, throwing her hands up, praising the Lord. He knew he needed what she had. But all the church members told him to say was "Oh Lord, save my soul."

This is how we entered into marriage, with no knowledge of Jesus Christ, and all the challenges the devil had prepared to break up our union. For many years, my husband sought after truth. He tried the Muslims, Jehovah Witnesses, Rev. Ike, and even the Georgia Prophet. He often tells about how he carried Rev. Ike's red rag in his pocket, and sent off for the Georgia Prophet's "blessed" powders.

Right about the time he decided to try the Prophet's powder (he actually sprinkled some dust in my shoes, he says), I decided that I had had enough. I left town for thirty days, and forbid anyone to tell where I was. He couldn't find me. Our marriage was in turmoil. I thought he was terrible, and I had no idea just how ugly I was myself. I considered myself a good person, and my ugly attitude seemed justified to me.

My husband had a fiery temper and I was stubborn. The submission taught in the Bible was a joke, an actual offense to me. I didn't want a man telling me what to do. What a pair. Then, my dear husband met Jesus. All alone, on the front porch of our home, he cried out: "God, if you are real, then show yourself." My husband went inside, sat on the edge of our bed, and there, in his solitude, God came to him, and revealed Jesus. Not just the story book Jesus, but the life changing Jesus.

After that life changing experience, my husband shoved aside all of his other books, on how to be rich and successful, on black power, astrology, and all other psychology and religion topics. He started reading the Bible, day in and day out. He played Kenneth Copeland tapes so much that I couldn't stand it. It didn't matter. He kept on reading and listening. I didn't believe it at first, I thought it was just another one of his schemes. But he kept on changing, or the Lord kept transforming his old sin nature.

Finally, one day, I began to want to change too. I wanted what he was getting. And so, I too gave my life to Jesus. Once my husband and I had both decided to serve the Lord, our whole life turned around. I wanted to be like the woman in Proverbs 31. We started going to Bible Study and a holiness church. I guess at first, my zeal carried me to the limits. For a while, I didn't wear lipstick,

59

didn't style my hair. I was hungry for the truth. As time went on, I began to grow up in the Word, to know that I am to be a beautiful example of God's love and grace. I began to share this good news with other women, to see their lives changed, and their marriages restored.

This was all very wonderful until God told my husband to leave his career and go full time into the ministry. Over the years, we had graduated from food stamps and an apartment, to high salaried positions, a lovely home, nice cars. I wasn't aware how important these things were to me, until the call came. I thought back to the day when my husband had demanded (after six months of food stamps) that we stop using welfare. "I am a man!" he insisted. "We will not live this way!" He always worked, but sometimes it had been hard to make it, so I had gotten the food stamps, without consulting him.

He hated eating cabbage and gristle hamburgers, but he hated food stamps even more. I am glad he did. Within a short period, he turned our circumstances around. This was early in our marriage. I guess as I reflected how God had delivered us from food stamps, I began to realize that I could trust Him to carry us into wherever He was leading us now.

The "wherever" continues to expand. God met our needs from the very moment we stepped out into the unknown. There were stormy moments. We have had to learn faith, and live by faith. But the fruit of the promise is real in our lives. We now have a beautiful marriage, three beautiful children who all live for the Lord, and an extended family as pastors of a church with a congregation of 2,000+.

I do not regret one moment of my life. The love that I share with my husband is more than I could ever have imagined. The Bible says that if I am a godly woman, I will do my husband good and not evil all the days of our life. I obey and submit to my husband as he submits to God. I do not feel ruled and dominated. I know that I am loved. My precious husband often says that I am his best friend. He truly is my best friend. Together, Jesus is the center of our joy. We go on together in Christ, from glory to glory.

May: Delight In The Lord

I had been married once. It ended in disaster. I was hurt, bruised, and didn't want to see another man, I thought, for as long as I lived. I was content to throw myself into God, and drown my sorrows in the heart of the "Breasty One."

Then, one day, I was sitting talking with my girlfriend. We were on the couch in the den. She exclaimed, "Oooh!" When I asked her what happened, she said, "A man just walked through your house, he has long legs, and he belongs here."

Now, there was no man in my house. At least, not that our natural eyes could see. Yet, she had seen someone. Not many days later, we visited a new church. When we sat down, just behind a good looking man, my friend dropped everything in her lap, and her eyes stretched large. "Oooh!" I pretended that I didn't see her or the man. But I saw him, and little did I know it, he saw me, too.

For many weeks my friend and I continued to visit the church. Often, we would sit near the man, and he began to come up to me after church and chat. He always sought me out. I never went after him. Our words were never intimate, neither were they suggestive, and yet we knew that we liked each other. I had purposed in my heart not to be forward. I knew that his ex-wife was a member of the same church, and had heard that many of the members were praying for their marriage to be restored.

It was all more than my friend could handle. She was so certain he was the man she had seen in my apartment. The more I admonished her to be patient, the more adamant she became. She couldn't understand why he was being so reserved. One night, without telling me, she called around until she found his phone number. She just called him up and asked him: "I know you like my friend. What is wrong with you? Do you have a Bible there?" When he said he had a Bible, she demanded that he read the story of Ruth to her on the phone. As soon as their three hour conversation was over, he called me, and we talked for almost seven hours straight. He came over to my house the next day. We were in each other's company constantly. Our relationship blossomed overnight. Things speeded up. The Lord resolved the issues that were standing in the way of our relationship developing, and we were married within months.

All the time that this remarkable relationship was coming together, I had purposed in my heart to focus on, to delight in God. I wasn't looking for a man. My desire was for things of God. In the back of my mind, and heart, I knew I wanted a mate, but I wouldn't allow that to be my focus. Because I wasn't desperate for a husband, I was able to attract one. He pursued me.

Even though there was a question of his former wife, and what would happen there, I found my position in God, and stood on it. I decided to trust in the Lord with all my heart and to lean not to my own understanding. As I acknowledged Him in all my ways, he directed my path into the arms of lasting love. Today, my husband and I are in ministry together. We understand God's plan for man and woman to be one. I am submitted to him, he covers me with his love. Together, we are overcoming in Jesus' name.

Belinda: The Wolf
in Sheep's Clothing

I was a career woman first. I had spent years getting an education and moving ahead in my chosen profession. During that process, I found the Lord, and career took a second seat. Still, I was not looking for a man, a husband. The Bible says that he who finds a wife finds a good thing. I guess I always expected to be found, so I didn't spend time looking. I dated on occasion, but was content with my life as it was.

Then came the season of a whirlwind courtship in my life. I had passed the point of thirty, and a man in our church congregation sought me out. I was cautious at first, but he was persistent in his pursuit. He wanted to spend almost every moment with me. We walked together, played tennis together, read the Bible together. He was warm, affectionate, loving, and appeared to be very godly. He never approached me in a lustful way, and yet, I believed that I was the desire of his heart.

He had been married before, but he blamed his wife for the rift. His wife was so bitter and hurt, that she added to his reports of her conduct by her hostile behavior. I had no reason to doubt him, because the leaders of our church were in full support of him, and had restored him to a position of respect in the body.

We planned a lavish wedding, everyone was jubilant. The ceremony was lovely. As soon as it was over, the nightmare began. We went on what was to be a romantic honeymoon, and on our wedding night, he withdrew from me as though I were a leper. He made it very clear, even as we became intimate in the days to come, that it was distasteful to him. He became snide, insulting and very cold and distant when we were alone together.

In public, it was a different story. He painted a picture to the church leaders that was unreal. He said that I was cold, calculating, had married him for his money, that I refused my marital duties. He would greet the congregation with warmth and cordiality, and turn to me with utter contempt in his eyes. He continued to portray me as a bitter, complaining woman. The church leaders believed him. It was like living with Dr. Jekyll and Mr. Hyde.

In name, we are still married today. We no longer live together and do not communicate. I do not have an explanation for this strange situation. I do know that there are real, God ordained mates, and counterfeit lovers. I would admonish all Christians to seek God with all your heart, when making a serious decision such as choosing a mate for life.

Alveda: A Personal Testimony

In 1983, I was called away from everything I had ever known. I had been born into a prominent family. My father, Rev. Alfred Daniel Williams King, and my mother, Naomi King, had no idea that they were bringing into the world a child that would one day grow up and declare out and out war on the devil, and have a burning desire to see black men, women and families saved from destruction and safely delivered into the family of God.

My grandfather, Dr. Martin Luther (Daddy) King, Sr., was a preacher. My uncle (Dad's brother), Dr. Martin Luther King, Jr., was a preacher and a world famous Civil Rights Activist. For many years, I longed to capitalize on what I considered to be the fame that was associated with my uncle and the accolades of the Civil Rights Movement.

During my lifetime, God graced me with many abilities. I am the mother of six wonderful children. I can sing, dance, write, hold degrees and certificates in Journalism, Business, Counseling, Paralegal, Art, Computers and other skills and abilities such as cooking and gardening. I have been a successful actress, a powerful state legislator; I was always very impressed with myself.

I was in for a very rude awakening. God was not impressed with me. There was too much of "I" and almost none of "Him" in my life. I wanted the spotlight. I wanted to be recognized for what I considered to be my accomplishments.

In 1983, a colleague of mine at Atlanta Metropolitan College, (where I have taught for ten years) asked me who Jesus Christ is. I had been baptized at the age of five, and really did believe that Jesus was born of the Virgin Mary, and that He had died on the cross at Calvary. But I didn't know Him. As she began to take me through the scriptures, John 3:16, Rom. 1, Rom. 10-9, and many others, I realized that there was something missing in my life that my Baptist Church experience, that my excursions into Buddhism, Transcendental Meditation, Muhammedism, and other pseudo-spiritual excursions had not provided.

About an hour into our conversation, I realized that Jesus Christ is really God. As I spoke those words aloud, a rushing hunger and desire filled me. I wanted more. And thus began my quest for a relationship with the living God.

I began to be aware of a closeness with God that I had never experienced during the very traumatic events of my life. To name a few:

1. My baby sister was severely burned when I was five.

2. During the Civil Rights Movement our home in Birmingham, Alabama was bombed while we were in bed sleeping.

3. I was drugged and arrested for demonstrating during the Civil Rights Movement.

4. My Uncle Martin (Dad's closest friend) was assassinated.

5. My Dad died mysteriously within months of the assassination.

6. I was married and divorced before I reached the age of twenty-five.

7. My dear grandmother was shot and murdered while playing the organ.

8. There were always death threats on my whole family.
9. My sister dropped dead while jogging.

All of these events occurred prior to 1983. Since that time:
1. My grandfather, who was my closest friend, died.
2. My mother's mother died.
3. My brother has dropped dead while jogging.
4. I have almost died several times myself.
5. I have been divorced the second time.

But there is one major difference. I no longer think that I am the center of my life, and I no longer desire to be recognized as the center of attention. I have experienced witchcraft attacks, physical and emotional abuse and many traumas, all of which I am convinced have strengthened me to fight the good fight of faith.

Life for me has been exciting, with great heights and depths. In my arrogance and ignorance, I grew to believe that the world owed me something. I remembered all the wrongs that had been done to me, and excused the wrongs that I had done to others. I was on a disaster course, even though it appeared that I had it all. Then, I met Jesus. He brought true joy and meaning to my life. Jesus brings balance to my life. I no longer seek thrills, I no longer experience great swings from joy to pain. Every moment with Jesus is a joy, even in the midst of trials.

Since 1983, there have been many experiences and events that brought me to this place. I have learned great principles and applied them to my life. God led me on a path to establish me in Him.

(1983) I received Jesus as my personal savior.

(1984) I was filled with the Holy Spirit

(1985) A woman whom I have known since early childhood came to my rescue when I needed to learn how to fight. Aunt A.

taught me to read the Bible and to call on Jesus. Ephesians 6, Psalms, especially 91, 37, 23, and 70 were a real blessing. Ecclesiastes, Psalm 139, and the Gospel of John remain my personal favorites. I joined Fellowship of Faith Church International and began to learn about Christian warfare.

(1987) God led me to a series of good, Bible teaching churches, until he planted me in my church home, Believers' Bible Ministry of Atlanta.

From 1983, on, I began to see and understand how I had allowed family status, material possessions, worldly fame and other influences to have preeminence in my life. I had looked to men for answers, while God was there all the time. I had even made my Uncle Martin into an idol in my life. I thought that doors would open in the name of Martin Luther King, Jr., even though Martin himself constantly wrote and spoke about the power of God being the solution to all of man's problems.

As I began to grow spiritually, I began to understand that man's problems are not with social ills. What we have identified as our enemies are just the manifestation of the devil's hatred of mankind. The devil has always wanted to destroy Abraham's (natural and spiritual) seed. Abraham's seed is the seed of promise. Abraham's seed produced Jesus, the Messiah. In Micah, there is a prophecy that the remnant of Jacob (Israel) shall be among the gentiles in the midst of many people as a lion among the beasts of the forest and the flocks of sheep. The devil wants to destroy all of Abraham's seed. Some of the weapons the devil uses to kill the seed of man are genocide in the form of:

1. Drugs: which wreak havoc on marriages, families and on individual lives. When men (and women) use drugs, it lowers their fertility, their moral standards, their potential to produce healthy children.

2. Crime: Crime leads to jail. In jail, the black man can neither produce nor provide for a family.

69

3. Abortion: In the last decade (eighties, early nineties) over ten million babies have been aborted in America alone. This is more deaths than previous wars. Many of those babies were products of black seed.

4. Homosexuality: Men loving men, and women loving women in sexual relationships cannot produce babies.

5. Sexual addictions: Sexual addictions lead to break up of families, and consequently have a destructive effect on those involved. Other sexual disasters include AIDS and other venereal diseases brought on by promiscuous sex.

These five factors are brought against the human race by the human race. People tend to use their God given right to choose in ways that bring detriment to themselves and their race. Add to these factors racism, societal pressures and other factors, and you have major enemies to the seed of man.

Somehow, we as women must understand our purpose. We must support life, and families. We deserve love, marriage, and relationships, but it must come according to God's plan and purpose. We must rediscover our roles.

Now, today and forever, my greatest desire is to forgive and to be forgiven, to love and grow in God, for Jesus Christ to be the center of my life, that all men see Jesus in me, that they may come to know Him intimately. I pray, in the name of Jesus, that this book, in some way, will draw you and all who read it, closer to the God of John 3:16. "For God so loved the world, that He gave His only begotten Son, Jesus, that whosoever believes on Him, shall not perish, but have everlasting life."

The Devil Is
A Real Enemy Who Can And
Must Be Defeated

With the advent of such movies as "The Exorcist," "The Omen," "Dracula," and more recently "Ghost," people have become more and more aware of a spirit world. The movie "Ghost" convinced even the unbelieving of a life after death. Remarkably, there has always been a spirit world. At the dawn of mankind, the angel Lucifer was kicked out of Heaven and became Satan. From that point on, he and the angels/demons who fell with him have existed to torment, tantalize, trick and tempt humankind into such a state, that they remain cut off from God forever.

In divine contrast, Jesus Christ was born, crucified and resurrected to circumvent and eradicate the plans and evil works of Satan. Jesus provides light and eternal life to all who choose to receive Him as their savior. Jesus is real, Satan is real. Earth is real, Heaven is real, and hell is real. Demons are real, and they exist today, and wreak great havoc in the lives of men, women and children. Demons communicate with humans via emotions. Therefore, we may think we are making a decision ourselves, when it is really a dark spirit compelling us. You may have heard the saying "The devil made me do it?" What does this really mean? Are there really spirits that affect our behavior? The answer is yes. Demons are real. God is also real and is bigger than any demon or devil. It is our goal to make the reader aware of demonic activity so that she or he can be free to experience true, fulfilling, godly relationships.

For the purpose of this book, we will study a demon spirit who is known as Jezebel. There was a woman, Jezebel, in Bible days who was very wicked. She had a spirit of control, dominance, witchcraft and rebellion that caused men to shake in their shoes. Often, today, women are labeled as Jezebels because they seduce men to danger and destruction.

In many instances, men seek out women with these controlling, Jezebel-like spirits, because the men feel that these women deserve to be mistreated. The men may already be angry with women, or a woman in particular, and are seeking out a woman to punish. A man will also feel less guilty in betraying a Jezebel type than a genuinely meek, submitted woman. A man planning to drink, carouse, commit adultery and misbehave and abuse in general may seek to marry a Jezebel so that he can rationalize (no matter how falsely or unjustly) that she is getting what she deserves when he mistreats her. Jezebel women are often attracted to these "Ahab" type men. Darkness attracts darkness, and such relationships lead invariably to unhappy, frustrated, disappointed lives.

Since demons do not have gender as we know it, the Jezebel spirit is not a female spirit, but women lend themselves more easily to its influence than men. Men tend to react more readily to an "Ahab" spirit, which reacts to Jezebel's control in fear, hostility, suspicion and anger, often manifesting in violence.

Some examples of the manifestation of this type of demonic activity are as follows:

A woman may tell her husband that a real man would make more money, or she may sigh and complain all the time about what they don't have. The man, fully aware and at a loss for not having what is expected, feels pressured. They begin to go at one another, each justifying his or her position. The man may try to prove his worth, or may give up and refuse to perform at all.

She may resort to bedroom blackmail, refusing to sleep with him until he produces what she wants. He may feel so degraded with the little, hostile sex she does allow, that he becomes turned off totally. He may respond by turning to t.v., newspapers, drink, drugs, or other women.

She may be bossy, or whining and complaining. She may pretend to be sweet and feminine and helpless, but in reality, she will be just as determined to have her way as he is.

Children brought up in this environment often grow up to be manipulators themselves. A rebellious mother often breeds rebellious children. The weakness of the father coupled with the dominance of the mother is confusing and upsetting to children.

The woman may try to become the spiritual headship of the home. If she finds the Lord first, she may try to make the husband and children come in line. The more she insists, the more he resists. This type of woman usually won't trust God to give her husband the wisdom and guidance to lead the family. As a result, the "Ahab" rises up and the man rebels.

Although the Bible says that we are all royal priesthood, a woman can afford and allow a man to lead the household, spiritually. If not, the husband may refuse God altogether. Too many tapes, books, showy prayers and testimonies often fail. Men have an inherent understanding that spiritual leadership is a responsibility assigned to them by God. An unbelieving husband is won (written in God's Word) by a quiet and obediently submitted wife. In order for a woman to receive her heart's desire, she must do the Word of God!

Here is a prayer which has been helpful to free many:

"Father, I come to you in the name of Jesus Christ, the Shepherd of my soul. I confess and renounce as sin everything I have ever done to manipulate, dominate and control other people. I hate and renounce the foul Jezebellic spirits and claim deliverance from them in Jesus' name (Psalm 139).

"Because Jesus died on the cross for my sins and lifted a curse from me, blotting out the handwriting of ordinances which were against me, I declare every curse having to do with the Jezebellic spirits to be broken from whatever source, even back to seven generations on both sides of my family.

"I also ask, Father, that You sever any ties of bondage which may exist between me and those who have practiced sorcery against me.

"Direct me to the undershepherd You have ordained for me, and above all else, help me to come into true submission to You, Father. Jesus said: 'Those who believe in Me, in my name shall cast out demons.' I am a believer, and in Jesus' name I now command all spirits associated with the Jezebellic influence to leave me now and set me completely free in Jesus' name. Amen."

—Based on a tract: *The Jezebel Influence* by Jim Croft

Forgiveness Vs. Debt Collecting

It is natural to expect someone who has wronged us to apologize and to make up for the wrong done. It is natural, but not God's way. We humans have a way of collecting debts and injuries, and holding people hostage until they magically understand what they have done wrong, and say and do all the right things (according to our wishes) to make it right.

It is hard to forgive because sometimes the persons we must forgive are wrong, mean, and hard-hearted. We have to accept and love those who hurt us, to release the wrong-doers. Just when we want to see them get what they deserve, the Word of God says to love them. We have to forget hurt, bitterness, pride and resentment, and *love* them. This is very hard. We want to repay wrong for wrong, rather than right the wrongs.

People have often confused forgiving with forgetting. Sometimes the pain is so deep that we cannot forget, or at least it would take a very long time to forget. Even if we forget our responses to the injury, like the anger and the pain, we may take forever to forget the actual injury. Sometimes we try to pretend that it never happened. This is denial. If we deny or overlook, the hurt will only fester, and the injury will grow deeper to a point of fatality, a death of heart if not body.

Anger is a powerful emotion that has to be dealt with honestly. Anger must be vented, ideally through prayer, rather than through natural and emotional means such as fighting and screaming.

Jesus is the perfect example in dealing with wrongs done to us. Jesus voluntarily took all of our hurts, pains and injuries in his own body on the tree of Calvary (I Pet. 2:21-24) to pay the debt of sin for all of us. As a result, anyone can be released from sin and guilt by accepting Jesus' gift. (Rom. 6:23, John 10:28-30). God dropped all charges, erased all debts, cancelled by the blood sacrifice of Jesus.

Forgiveness springs from God's grace and unconditional love. He forgave us through Jesus that we might love and forgive others. Through the Holy Spirit, we grow in the fruits of the spirit. Meekness, a fruit which increases as we practice forgiveness, leads to gentleness. Once all of our energies are focused and directed by love and gentleness, God can use us for His glory.

Once we develop in these areas, God can use us for His good, and we will not resist Him. His love will be reflected through us in our dealings with those who mistreat, insult or abuse us in any way. We can endure in patience without negative reactions. We will bear one another's burdens, and enter into the mystery of Christ's sufferings.

Unforgiveness, bitterness, and resentment are deadly to the spirit, soul, and body. Diseases such as cancer and arthritis are linked to these hostile emotions. The fruit of these deadly attitudes are far more costly than they are worth.

Bitterness

If God's grace is not applied to a hurt, then a root of bitterness sets in. If the wound does not heal, then there is evidence of bitterness, a wound in the spirit (Proverbs 18:14). We must apply God's grace (Heb. 12:15), we must forgive (Matt. 6:14-15; 7:1,2; 18:21-35) and thank God for all things (Eph. 5:20; Phil. 4:6).

Sometimes, we try to forgive those who hurt us, but memory recall keeps us rehearsing past events, and we keep longing for them to pay us, or we long to pay them back for the wrongs they have done. Every time we remember, the old pain and anger flood back in. This is a sure sign that bitterness is present, and is unhealed. In order to be free from this bitterness, we must forgive and receive God's grace and His comfort.

Vengeance belongs to God; He will repay (Heb. 10:30). We cannot carry such heavy burdens; Jesus said he would carry our burdens. God has promised to pay; it is His job, not ours. Forgive and do not condemn those who wrong you. Jesus has not condemned us for our sins; we are pardoned, so we must pardon.

We must turn to God for comfort. He must be the focal point, not the hurt, the pain, and the offender. We must allow the Holy

Spirit to comfort us. Therein we find peace that passes all understanding. We must forget ourselves, stop trying to work our way
out of things, even good works, and just lose ourselves in God's
love, grace, and mercy.

Sin And Iniquity

The scripture, "The wages of sin is death, the gift of God is eternal life," is often quoted, but is more often glossed over and virtually ignored. People tend to do what they want to do, and rely on God's grace. Little attention is given to the principle of reaping and sowing. Even though God's mercy and grace are sufficient to sustain us, we often have to eat the bitter fruit of our own seeds sown.

Although the words *sin* and *iniquity* are interchanged in our conversation, there is a need to understand what sin is and what iniquity is. Sin is the wrong thought or act. Iniquity is the cause. Sin is the bitter fruit. Iniquity is the foul fertilizer. Sin tends to be more current, something that we do in day to day living. Iniquity is generational.

We are born into sin and born in and of iniquity. There are at least 230 citations of the word iniquity in the Bible. God speaks of iniquity of three and four generations in many instances. Sin and iniquity cause us to make mistakes of serious consequence. We lose our iniquity and cease to sin as we are washed in Christ's blood, washed in God's word, and go through fiery trials of life. As we yield to God, and allow Him to have his way, rather than following our own prideful paths, we lose that fleshly, carnal, sinful nature and become more like Christ.

Many of the sins and the iniquity that caused the women in this book so much pain are sins of the heart, ie. covetousness, jealousy, hatred, and bitterness. The section on Forgiveness and Bitterness can help you to resolve much of that pain. Another type of sin and iniquity that must also be overcome is sexual sin.

Sexual Sins

Often our past keeps us in bondage. Sexual sins are a great barrier to spiritual freedom, and more recently men *and* women have fallen into a sexual revolution of such magnitude that even young people are extremely promiscuous. People are convinced that they should "sample the goods" before they commit to marriage. More often than not, this leads to more sampling in other pastures. The "sowing of wild oats" causes wilder harvest. The more sex one gets outside of God-ordained marriage, the more such promiscuous sex one desires. God's plan is love, marriage and sex. They come in that order. Anything else is counterfeit, and leads to great pain and disaster.

Freedom From Sexual Torment

Just as the wicked spirits of Jezebel and Ahab cause so much havoc in male/female relationships, there are evil spirits that torment susceptible people unmercifully. *Incubus* spirits attack females, *succubus* spirits attack men. These spirits are connected with the spirit of lust, and are associated with lust and experimentation with sexual sin (any sex outside of the holy bond of matrimony).

You may recall having erotic dreams, a sensation of lovemaking in your sleep, even to the point of being touched and caressed. Often, memory recall of passion experienced in a sexual relationship causes people to fantasize to such a point that they feel as though they are re-experiencing the relationship.

A person involved in such activities can eventually become a slave to lust. It is so tragic that these influences are constantly loosed on our young people in television, music, videos, print media, and films. Sexual addiction is becoming increasingly prominent at all levels and at all ages of society.

It is important to remember, however, that once we are free from sex sin or any sin and torment, we must change our conversation and our associations. If we will be tempted by our old haunts and friends—and surely we will be—we must learn to pray for those still in bondage, but to stay away from temptation until God equips us to go back into the land to rescue those who are still in torment. This prayer can help to free you from sexual sins and torment.

"Heavenly Father, I come to you in the name of the Lord Jesus Christ. I believe that he is the Son of God who takes away the sin of all those who repent and confess Him as Lord. I believe that the blood of Jesus Christ cleanses me from all sin. I claim freedom from all filth of a sexual nature which came through my eyes, my ears, my mind, or through actual participation in sin.

"In particular I confess the following: all preoccupation with sensual desires and appetites, and indulgences of them; all longing and ardent desire for what is forbidden (evil concupiscence); all inordinate affection, all unnatural and unrestrained passions and lusts; all promotion or partaking of that which tends to produce lewd emotions and foster sexual sin and lust.

"I further confess all filthy communication; obscene and filthy language, conversation and jokes; lewd and obscene music, poetry, literature and art; all pornography; all acts of sodomy, adultery, immorality, fornication, masturbation, oral sex, effeminacy and homosexuality; also all affection for and attachment to philosophies, religions, and life-styles which glorify, promote, and condone sexual conduct in thought, word and deed contrary to the standard for believers in the Bible.

"I further renounce the expression of these philosophies, religions, and life-styles in art, literature, mass media, and public practices and attitudes. Lord, I ask that your Spirit reveal other sexual offenses in my life that I have committed.

"Father, I confess and renounce all occult involvement, both known and unknown, by me or my ancestors. I hate Satan, his demons, and all his works; I count all that offends you, Father, as my enemy (Psalm 139:21-24).

"Your Word declares: 'In my name shalt they cast out devils. . .' (Mark 16:17); 'I give unto you power . . . over all the power of the enemy, and nothing shall by any means hurt you' (Luke 10:19). Jesus came '. . .to destroy the works of the devil,' and to 'turn them (men) from the power of Satan to God' (I John 3:8; Acts 26:18). I accept these promises and in Jesus' Name, command Satan and all his hosts of evil spirits to come out of me, body, mind and spirit. Especially I renounce the following spirits of sexual sin: (Insert here names of specific sexual sins you have committed).

"I also renounce the Prince of Occult Sex and command all of his demons to leave me now in the name of Jesus Christ my Savior.

"Christ was made a curse on the cross for me (Galatians 3:13) and blotted out the handwriting of ordinances against me (Colossians 2:14). I declare all curses over my life, whether through my own sins or those of my ancestors, to be broken; particularly in the area of sexual sin and occult involvement. I claim freedom from all curses which have been placed upon me in the name of Jesus Christ.

"I hereby reclaim all ground that I have ever give to Satan in body, mind, soul, or spirit. I dedicate it to you Dear Lord, to be used for Your glory alone. I want you to control and empower every area of my life, including all my sexual powers; that from now on they might be used according to Your will. I also now give to You my affections, emotions and desires, and request that they might be motivated and controlled by Your Holy Spirit (Romans 12:1,2). Amen."

From *Conquering The Hosts of Hell* by Win Worley. Reprinted with permission of the author.

Fuchia: Rediscovering The Purpose Of The Woman

*Author's note: The following are excerpts from notes taken at a conference I attended, the **International Third World Leaders Conference 1992 Summit** REDISCOVERING PURPOSE. I am including these segments, because I believe there are "nuggets" of great value which will help in understanding more of God's plan and desire for the very best of life.*

This presenter talked about how God had named her Magdeline, although her daddy allowed her mother to include Magdeline as a second name. The daddy always insisted that her name was Magdeline, even though she went by her first name. The speaker was an older woman, full of wisdom.

She said the church world as we know it has taken the fallen doctrine of the church (men ruling over women) and attempted to make it into Divine Order. Going back to Genesis, she told how God cursed Adam and Eve by causing Adam to rule over Eve, and turning Eve's desire away from Him (God) to her husband

Adam, thereby causing a longing and emptiness that Adam was never designed nor created to fulfill. Only Jesus can satisfy a longing soul. Unredeemed men rule, redeemed men lead.

God does not operate by gender, rather He operates by and through the anointing. The prophet spoke that in the latter days sons and daughters would prophecy. We are spirit beings, some of us are housed in female bodies. In the spirit there is no gender.

The first evangelist after the death and resurrection was a woman, Mary Magdeline.

The husband is truly the priest of the home, as it is written. It is also written that we are all royal priesthood, a chosen generation. Therefore we are priests in the home. The husband is the head or the leader over the home, not the only royal member. God has seven realms of authority here on earth. None of them overlap nor contradict.

Unless the husband is also the pastor of a congregation, he is the authority over the home, not the church. Women should never use as a reason, "My husband won't let me go to church." Suppose you are driving a car, and your husband is on the passenger side, and commands you to speed because you are in a hurry. You do not agree, but submit to his authority anyway. When the police stops you, he will want your driver's license, not your husband's. You will be expected to answer for your decisions. We must follow our husbands as they follow Christ. If the husband demands immoral behavior or behavior contradictory to the Word of God, we must obey God rather than man. The man, as head of the house, is subject to Jesus.

We must become mature, able to comprehend more of God's nature, and assume more of God's character. Jesus reached maturity in His life and His ministry here on earth. Adam and Eve never reached maturity because they allowed rebellion to hinder them. Their basic sin was independence, not depending on and obeying God. This was even worse than just disobeying. They separated themselves from Him by an independent act.

God made us so he could pour himself into us. He wants us to develop an understanding of sonship and throneship. Everyone who gets breath doesn't get eternal life. Some will live an eternal death in hell. In an intertheistic covenant, God made arrangements for us to live with Him, but we must surrender our will.

The tree of good and evil included humanism, atheism, skepticism, communism, new age, women's lib, and every other evil that we can imagine, and some that we can't.

Eve was named after the fall; she was redeemed so that she could bring seed that would eventually destroy the devil. God drove Adam out of the garden; Eve followed. God did not command her to go; she loved and needed her husband.

The next supreme battle and attack from Satan will be deception. Satan stole Eve, God's first bride, through deception, and now he's coming after the second bride, the church, through deception. The only difference is, Adam was not God; Jesus is and is well able to protect His bride. The second Adam (Jesus) will deliver His bride safely.

We must continue to overcome Satan. He was cursed to crawl on his belly and eat dust. Our frames are dust, and we must remain covered by the Word, in order to be protected from his devouring tactics.

As for Eve's turning to her husband, women need to be redeemed from the curse, and be turned towards Jesus. God doesn't expect a man to meet your spiritual needs. A man cannot. You inner sanctuary is God's home. It is a curse to desire/turn to a man outside of the order ordained in marriage. We are to love our husbands and live for God.

Fallen men rule, redeemed men lead. When your inner sanctuary is controlled by a man, a man rules over you. This does not mean that a man cannot be an effective leader of his home. When we return or are redeemed from the fall, God comes to live in us, and we by His nature in us, become submissive.

Everything is easier when God rules and reigns. His hand is tempered with love and mercy towards those who love Him and obey Him. Consider, even work is lighter in countries who love the Lord, and trials are fewer.

Women are the carriers of the seed who will crush Satan's head. The church (feminine form) will marry the Son Christ.

Men in the flow of God are not domineering men. They are powerful, yet meek, gentle, kind men. We are then our husband's reflections. If they are godly, we are expressions and extensions of that godliness. We do not rule, override or argue with them; we submit to them as they submit to Christ. As they become God's expressions, they allow God to express Himself through us.

A Testimony of Two Men

Author's note: This is recorded as told by two men. Their voices interchange.

Voice One:

I met her as the seasons were changing. She walked with a sureness of purpose. Her beauty was not so much physical as spiritual. Her face was radiant. I approached her, and she was warm, yet aloof, if such a thing is possible. I commented on her smile, and said something like, "I wish I was the man who makes you smile." She asked, "How do you know that a man put this smile here?" I responded, "I am a man, I know."

During the course of this first meeting, she told me that there was a man, but that their relationship was not romantic, and probably never would be. She thought she loved him, but that it was a love that God had not ordained. I was sure that she was right, because I knew then that she was my spiritual wife. I also knew this other man was an absolute fool if he let her get away without a fight. I was involved with another woman, and was deeply enmeshed in a physical bond, and yet I knew this woman standing before me was to be forever a part of my life. I was willing to fight to have her.

And yet knowing that she had been given to me, I knew that this man we were talking about and this woman I was bonded to were not out of the picture by a long shot. She, this lady of the changing seasons, was naive on these points. She knew nothing about this woman I was involved with, and was fooling herself about the man she thought she could walk away from.

Over the course of a few months, I found myself drawn closer and closer to my spiritual wife. I would continue to tell her that she was mine before the foundations of the world. She was drawn to me and would not admit that this other man was still a part of her life. Theirs was a bond that I understood. Flesh and soul are powerful entities that we all contend with. She continued to deny her battle; I continued to wage mine. She was perceptive enough to discover my relationship with the woman who had ensnared me. Sometimes the lady of light and life, as I think of her, would become jealous and irrational, which embarrassed her. She couldn't contend with her emotions, which she had suppressed for many years.

Once in awhile, when she would speak of this other man, she would say that he and I were so close in the spirit that we were like siamese twins. She couldn't tell us apart. She couldn't tell which of us was the "real one." It was times like these when I wanted to tell her, just go to him. I knew that she needed me. I also knew that she was going to have to face the reality of her flesh and soul and will, before we could truly come together. Often, I would tell her to go to him and make love with him. After all, I rationalized, the only way to deal with flesh is to jump straight into it. In truth, I was still battling my own flesh bond with the woman I was involved with. It was easier to deal with the possibility of my lady of light turning to him, than to loose this other woman's hold on my life. The new relationship was obtainable, at a price. The current relationship was comfortable and enticing. I was familiar with matters of the soul and flesh. Until I met my life's mate, I was content after a fashion. There is a high price for obtaining a true eternal relationship. Many times I had cried out to God to give me my spiritual woman, my wife. I had known God well during my life. Sometimes I walked with God; sometimes I had walked away. When I met her, I knew that I was ready to come back to God for good. I knew that I could have what God wants for me with the woman I met as the seasons changed.

I knew that I couldn't take her as I had taken countless women before her. Ours could not be a union of flesh and soul alone. At first, she told me this same thing, that ours would have to be a spiritual relationship. In her mind and heart, she understood this. She had underestimated her passions and her flesh. There quickly came a time when I had to draw away from her. It was apparent that we were so compatible, that she had as much a challenge resisting me, as I had resisting her. Almighty God Himself told me not to touch her too soon, or all would be lost.

I could not use the power, the charm, the magnetism that I had used to draw so many women to me. My voice, my intellect, my mannerisms, my appearance were given to me to attract people to the kingdom of God. In rebellion, I had often used these gifts to seduce women. Now, it was all turned against me. I had met my match, the counterpart of all that I am. And I could not use any of my natural abilities to claim her. She, with the voice, and mind, and body that can turn a man's whole being in her direction, was forbidden to join with me at this time. Ours was the temptation that Adam and Eve faced, to know what was currently forbidden, to touch and experience what was only to come within the acceptable scope of God's plan. To take this woman to my body before God's time was a desire that I had to overcome.

It was almost too much to see her and not touch her. So, I began to pull away from her. She resisted out of her stubborn will. She was determined to keep me close. I was determined to do God's will. This trial between us forced her to submit further to her God and Master. She did not like it, but she surrendered to the will of the Father. In kind, I began to yield to God myself. I began to hear His voice, His plans for my life. I knew that I had to shield her and yield my life at the same time.

Voice Two:

It was during this season that she turned to me. She was vulnerable, and I knew it. She had told me about him, soon after she met him. I didn't believe her, because I knew that she was falling in love with me. I was confident. I knew that she was special. I didn't know what I wanted from her, but I wanted her. I too had known the voice of God. I had accepted Jesus Christ as my Lord, and yet, after walking with Him for a season, had turned again to my own way.

When I met her, it was a tantalizing experience. She is beautiful in many ways. In truth, I wanted her body, first, before I began to know her. When I first met her, she ran from me. Later, she told me her attraction to me frightened her. She was determined to resist me; I was determined to have her.

When first I tried to woo her to me, she prayed very hard and God intervened. Our rendezvous was interrupted by the hand of God. It shook me so that I told her that we would have to be friends. She accepted this, and continued to be my friend. She would often give me scriptures and inspirational gifts that pricked my conscience, a will I thought was hardened to things of God.

And yet, every time I would see her, I wanted more and more of her. She would speak of him, this "husband" she had met, and yet, I thought he was someone she had made up to cover the hurt of my rejection. And then one day, for some reason, I believed her. There was another man. I was surprised, and realized that someone was taking her away from me. I did not want to let her go, and so, even though God had warned me to leave her alone, I went after her again.

Probably because this other one had withdrawn from her, at least his physical presence, she was not so strong. She was lonely, longing for her husband. Even though I knew that I was not him, I pursued. She began to talk with me, and once again, was drawn to me. I was relentless. I pursued her. She resisted, and yet, I did not give up. She would pray, and yet, I pursued. I must admit, it was a game for me. She knew it, and yet, because it was her season for temptation, she was drawn to me.

Somehow, God used her to touch me. At her weakest moments, when she would pray, and God would hear her, and move for her, *I* was moved. I felt wrong. I was going after something that wasn't mine. I was after her for the wrong reasons. I wanted her; I admired her. I missed her when she wasn't near, and would draw her to me. I even considered marrying her, just to serve my own desires and purposes. And yet, she prayed for me. She loved me. She resisted me, as best she could.

She told me that God had shown her my heart. A proud and arrogant heart, a cynical heart, and yet a heart of strength and valor. She knew that if she failed God and me, that I would turn away from God again. She wanted more than anything for me to come back to God.

My battle has never been with her. In my own way, I love her. I have never met another like her. She is warm, strong, intelligent, giving, and very passionate. I could walk with a woman like this. She does not compete with me; she compliments me. She loves me without motive and expectations other than that I return to God.

Many times I have tried to make her fall away from the grace that she clings to; to leave the righteous path and turn to carnal reality. She resists, sometimes in strength and sometimes in a weakness so appealing and shattering that I am ashamed and am brought to my knees in remorse and repentance. Even while I have been determined to conquer her, I have prayed that she will remain strong and true to her God. Even while I am certain that there are no true Christian women who cannot be wooed and seduced away from their talk of holiness, I pray that she is real, and that her faith is true.

My quest for her in actuality is a challenge to God to prove that He is real and that there are people who really do live for Him, and who are changed by His power. I see Jesus in her. I am drawn to Him by her love. God forgive me for not believing. God help me to become what I must be.

She Speaks:

God help me, for I have loved them both. They are so strong, and so beautiful to me. In them, I see the promise of what God intends for our black men to be. I am almost sure that he, the one who speaks first, is my "husband." There is such a joy and a completion for me in belonging to him.

I know that I can not belong to them both, in a Biblical sense. A woman must be wife to only one man. And so, one must be my friend and brother, while the other, I will submit to and walk with all our days. This is a joyous expectation for me.

The greatest challenge is to set aside even this intense desire to belong to my husband, for the reality of belonging to God forever. God is such a jealous God, that even a love like the love

93

between man and wife takes a back seat to the eternal, divine love of the father for his own. And to be God's own is the ultimate for me.

During this, my season of great temptation, waiting for the Father's will to be accomplished is my greatest challenge. I long for great truth, great peace, and great submission to my true Lord and Master. To be owned by God, to be completely cared for by Him, is the only way I will be satisfied. My husband will understand this driving need, and this need will be mirrored by my soul mate's own hunger for surrender to the Master. Only a man powerful enough to surrender to the Lord God, will be strong enough to win me to his side.

Iniquity and the driving passions of the flesh are real, and are to be reckoned with. They can only be overcome by much prayer, and the power of the Blood of Jesus and The Holy Spirit. In the process of overcoming, we must never give way to guilt, condemnation, and the yielding to sin. When sin comes, it must be overcome, oftentimes with great pain and suffering. I am no stranger to transgression. The most frightening aspect of falling away from God's grace is the loss of fellowship with Him.

The only way back to God's side is immediate repentance, and the turning away from that which causes us to falter. We must overcome our own lusts. When we are faced with the decision of whether to sin or to stay with the Father, we almost feel that we will die if we do not do the thing that leads us to sin and damnation. It is in these intense moments of conflict and pain, that we actually draw closer to God when we make the right choice. He truly never leaves us, nor forsakes us. We must believe this, and chose life!

There are times when my body literally screams out and demands a caress, a touch, a fleeting satisfaction. My soul cries out for tender words, and my imagination wants to plummet to pits of damnation. These feelings and emotions would exalt themselves against the knowledge and the very Word of my powerful Father. It is times like these when I must fight with all that is within me and cast down those high and heady thoughts and desires. There have been times when I did not succeed, and the price was not worth it. The pain and the guilt simply outweighed any temporary pleasure.

Do not think it strange when you go through these challenges. They come to rock your faith. Be strong in the Lord and in the power of His might. Keep yourself clothed in the helmet of Salvation, armed with the sword of the Spirit (God's Word), the breastplate of Righteousness, the girdle of Truth, the sandals of the Gospel of Peace, the shield of Faith, the robes of Humility, the garments of Praise, the mantle of the Anointing of Heaven, and the ornament of Grace. Never be caught naked. It is a frightening and deadly experience!

I encourage you, my Christian brothers and sisters, to press on for the mark of the highest calling. We can overcome the temptations of life. The fiery trials do not have to overtake us. Fight on, in the name of our Lord Jesus Christ.

Jim and John: What a Man Really Wants from a Woman

Devotion, loyalty, submission: Dirty words in today's society. I remember reading books about an imaginary planet called Gor, where the women couldn't even eat without the males' permission. Barbaric? I guess so. The image of the cave man dragging the woman around by the hair is far fetched, I know. But secretly, a man wants to dominate a woman. This domination is a natural desire, stemming from the curse in the Bible, where Adam and Eve were ousted from the Garden of Eden, and Eve was left totally dependent on Adam. I can imagine that Adam was pretty angry with Eve, even though he was still in love with her. The woman had the man by the nose, and yet she had given her loyalty away, by being beguiled by that stinking serpent.

Eve betrayed Adam's confidence by listening to someone else, and falling for a pretty line. By agreeing to eat the forbidden fruit, Eve cost Adam everything. Why didn't Adam disown Eve, and refuse to eat the fruit himself, and leave her to her own consequences? Adam was in love with the woman. He wanted to protect her, and share in her fate. Even though he tried to pass the blame on to her once the dirty deed was done, Adam did partake of Eve's sin. Adam wanted to remain one with his wife. She was a part of him, a vital part. Eve was Adam's heart, his sensitivity. Without Eve, Adam was not complete. The Bible says that a man will love his wife as his own body. No man hates his own body.

That's why men get so angry when women put church, family, friends and job ahead of them. We don't mind that God is the center of our woman's life. God should be the head. But after God, we should come first. We want a woman who is primarily (if not solely) interested in helping us to do, be and accomplish what we are about. This may seem selfish, but that's how God planned it. God designed women to be our helpmeets. When women step out of this role, and begin to compete, we see red! A man will do anything for a woman who supports him. But if that support is not there, we become reactionary. We might bury ourselves in our work, or worse, immoral activities. This is no excuse, God holds us accountable for our own actions, but this is how we feel. It is so disappointing to desire the real thing and get something fake. We often just give up, and settle for temporary, carnal gratification. This type of activity is never permanent, and it doesn't satisfy us. It just makes us more and more discontented with women. We are looking for something real, not fake.

We can also tell when a woman is faking it, when the devotion is counterfeit, not from the heart, but motivated by ulterior motives. For instance, if a woman gives us great sex in exchange for furs, houses, diamonds, etc., we know. We settle for what we get, but we are always desiring more. We do not want sex slaves, just a woman who is real, who satisfies our whole being. Maybe this is too much to expect, especially when we men are so angry with the world in general that we have very little to give in return.

We men, once we know Jesus Christ as our Lord and Savior, don't want to rule and dominate our women. We don't want to hurt them. We want to love, trust, and cherish our women. This doesn't mean that we want to put them in a box and keep them from careers and ministry calls. We just want everything other than God to be second for them, to come after us. If women could just understand this, and fit into this mode, they would see men change for the good. A man responds to healthy devotion. Not manipulation, and control, just good, honest love and support and concern.

As men, we have been so disappointed so many times, that we don't trust women anymore. We decide to hurt others before *we* are hurt. Women probably feel the same way, so you have a bunch of hurt, angry males and females tearing away at each other throughout eternity. How can it all stop? With some honest soul searching, and some real effort at trying to be what God wants us to be. We want to be real men. We need God to teach us, and we need our women to love us and believe in us. Without this, we are animals.

A Gentleman Speaks

We must have first in our lives, divine desire (Mk. 11). Broken vessels come today to be sealed up for things of the future. Desire for God will erase all pain of any hurt we have received. Our desire cannot be for things, cannot be for ministry, but our desire must be for God. We cannot afford to commit adultery with Jesus Christ's wife, who is the church. We must tend to our families and trust God to direct us as to how much time to spend with His wife. Preachers and pastors who spend more time with their ministries than with their wives/husbands and families are committing spiritual adultery (Gen. 2:21-25, Matt. 19:3, Tit. 2:4-5, Rom. 1:2, Prov. 24:3).

From the beginning, it was not so. Marriage is a creation ordinance. God is the author of marriage. God puts marriage on the road; man puts marriage on the rocks.

Some forms of Families recognized by society today:
1. Christian (Bible) type marriages
2. Common Law (Shacking)
3. Companion Union (Can include other than heterosexual relationships)
4. Disintegrate Union (visiting relationships from one woman/man to another)

Three factions that have altered the Bible way of families in the black family:
1. African Retention: polygamy or multiple wives
2. Plantation system: stud and breeding system which does not allow the man to be husband or father
3. Socio-economic-political factors: i.e., crime, homosexuality, abortion, education, finances

God ordained marriage in creating the union between Adam and Eve. Christ approves of marriage, and compares marriage of man and woman to His marriage to the church.

The purpose of marriage is to produce and raise up godly seed.

Another purpose of marriage is for *helpmeets*. Partners in marriage help each other to realize their dreams, to birth their visions.

Marriage is three faceted.
1. Public, whereby a man publicly leaves his family and takes a wife.
2. Permanent, in that the husband and wife cleave to each other.
3. Private, in that they join together in spirit, soul, and body (sexually) to become one.

(In-laws must respect God's order, and follow the word, or in-laws become out-laws.)

In order to experience this godly kind of marriage, we must go back to the beginning and rediscover God's plan and purpose for marriage. We must learn to govern ourselves and agree with this plan rather than to stubbornly cling to independence which cannot work in a marriage.

Poetry

All selections by Alveda King.

Whispering softly, love comes into my dreams
Shadow kissed by stardust, dancing with moonbeams.
Robed in promise of eternal delight
The mystery of love unfolding in the night.

Shadow touched by moonlight tender
True love's kiss awakened heart of slumber
King of Kings and Lord of Lords, the center
Of the love this life proclaims.

For an instant my world trembled
From a touch that came too soon
Steady, heartbeat. Listen. Listen.
For the sun has kissed the moon.

Father, dear, reveal your plan.
Jesus, you're my life, my joy.
Spirit, tender, Holy, guiding.
Dare I love this mortal man?

You Lord God are majestic splendor,
Clothed in excellence divine.
Oh may our love forever please you.
May our will be ever Thine.

Grant to us your peace, your power.
Not in our own strength, but thine.
Make us true and sure and earnest.
Lacking nothing, pure and fine.

You are the kingdom and the glory.
May your love be our life story.
And forever we will sing.
Of your mercy, God, our King!

Politics Can Make You . . .

Mad
Powerful
Excited
Politics can shape you; Politics can break you
Politics can woo you—to spend and *win*
Politics can make you. God! Don't let it *take* you
Body
Soul
Spirit
or politics can make you
a political animal.

Voices

You gave life voice
    To sing sweet psalms.

Life sings of degradation.

You gave life ears
    to hear your music

Life listens to pagan drums.

Life has many voices Lord.
    We need to only listen.

Of all the voices in my life
    Yours is sweetest.

Where Is Passion?

We crave a passion, hot and burning
We long for love, forever yearning

Our flesh deceives us, our loins mislead us
The path of throbbing passion calls us

Where is the joy of love? Nay, lust
leaves us crawling in the dust

103

Panting, wanting, needing, pleading
Forever searching, not succeeding.

Until submission, sure and lasting,
leads us to the source of power

Power, pleasure, joy; Yes Passion
Wait for us behind the door. When we yield
we know forever, love yes love,

Forevermore.

Big Momma

It's yo' show, Big Momma.
At least that's what they call you, ain't it,
With yo' minks, and lynx, and diamond studded sphinx,
You strut 'round like some reincarnated Nefertiti.
If someone were to ask you 'bout the Virgin Birth,
(You've given birth befo', but y'ain't no virgin.)
Would you say, "Virgin?" How unfashionable, Virgins
went out with the bite from that passion fruit, back there,
In the Garden, all those years ago.
Where, in the world,
Can you find a virgin these days?
I sure would like to sink my fangs—
Excuse me—*teeth*
Into
A Virgin.
Does this turn our mind to blood covenants? Occult violations?
Blood spilled out and sucked up over the centuries.
Blood untold, blood washing away the sins of the world?
The covenant Blood of the Lamb?
Maybe this is a dream. A fantasy.
A motion picture slice from the mind of a dreamer
Seeking eternity in the arms of
Her Savior
Where yo' gonna go?
I don't know
It's yo' show,
Big Momma.

Big Daddy

And what about you,
Big Daddy?
Forgetting wife,
And life,
And family, chasing dreams, making schemes
To out so
Slew
Foot.
Your master plan is to beat the odds
Play the game, make a name
For yourself.
After all, you grown ain't you?
Old Slew Foot cain't possible get one up
On you.
What you got to do
Is to make enough to buy yo' way out
Of that six foot deep dirt lined condo
Waitin' for you down the way.
Say . . .
The possibility of power; faith Shields,
Spirit Swords, seems
Ridiculous. Doesn't it?
Like seeking Him while He's findable?
Unrighteous acts can be bindable,
You know?
Anyway, who is He? You can't see Him, or touch
Him.
Although some nuts say they can actually feel Him.
Cain't rightly claim to know Him, huh?
But you do know old Slew Foot, don't you?
Lord of rejection, jealousy, murder . . .
Satisfy, gratify, the master of the flesh.
Love, family, joy, peace, must all be sacrificed on
Slew Foot's alter.
Witch's Brew, Occultish whispers
Drown out the sound of
angel"s wings.
Demonic voices, offer choices,
Porn and lust, and angel dust.
The mark of the beast appears
on the souls
Of our nearest and dearest . . .
friends?

Be for real! There is a way out,

you know.
His word is food
His word is drink.
His word is power.
The price? Your pride.
Laid aside. Cleansed by the
Blood of the Lamb.
Who is He?
Old Slew Foot knows.
What you gone do?
Big Daddy.

Ripples (In Time and Space)

Libations, fluids rippling on the sands bringing time and space together;
Bringing souls and spirits together . . . pebbles on the water, water making ripples,
Ripples in time.
"Behold I shew you a mystery; We shall not all sleep, but we shall all be changed
In a moment, in the twinkling of an eye, at the last
trump; For the trumpet shall sound, and the dead shall be raised
Incorruptible
And we shall be changed."

II

Libations, shadows rippling on the sand
The earth beneath my feet changes from my dark and musky
Mother, becoming red and alien, harsh,
As the waters ripple and the great ship rolls.

III

I am carried away from my familiar jungle of fruits and passion flowers, wild
animal friends and even wilder beasts;
Four legged animals, predators and yet, magnificent creations of God, with
Skins and furs . . . and *fangs.*

IV

Yet, change carries us over waters that no longer
Ripple
The water becomes an awesome, rolling jungle of waves
That carry us on in the Middle Passage
Washing us away from our home ground to a new land of tears and sorrow,
Our newfound home in a new world.

V

And yet, wherever we were bought,
Beaten and scattered, over continents and islands,
New blood was added to our veins; and yet the Blood of our Motherland remained,
True and deep.
In our new world, we learned to harvest new crops;
Some not quite so different from our jungle fruits and vegetation.
We tamed fields of cotton and tobacco
Even as our wild, free spirits were tamed by the new predator;
Two-legged beasts, still creatures of God, and not quite so magnificent in their
borrowed skins and furs.
But still their fangs, though changed
Remain *deadly*.

VI

The libations continue
The spirits that were summoned bring new birth to memories
Reflections of time itself.
We see ourselves in a new jungle still a part of God's creation,
And yet, the earth has changed.
The soil is not dark and musty between our bare and braceleted feet,
Nor is it red and cracked beneath our chained and callous feet.
It has become rock, concrete,
A machine-made improvement on nature,
And yet still part of nature.

VII

The tribal dancers before the sun, the wind, the rain and the Moon
have become whirling disco bodies beneath a myriad of simulated starlight,
lightning and thundering electrophonic sounds.

VIII

The hunter's spears and darts have become a mania for *Money*;
And guns bring down men and prey upon the weak who are Homeless, Jobless, and
Dreamless.

XI

The savagery continues, though times and methods change.
Humankind has changed, and yet has not changed, only
Shimmered and rippled in the reflections of time.

X

For though one generation passeth away, another generation
cometh. As the sun rises, it sets only to rise again.
The wind goes to the south only to return to the north,
Whirling continually, returning again according to its

circuits. And the rivers run to the sea, yet the sea is not full,
For the rivers return again to that place from which they came.
For that which has been, shall be again, and that which has been done,
Shall be done again.
For as all things change, they remain because: "There is no new thing under the sun."
There are only
Rippling images of change, all belonging to the universe, the Old, the New
created by the Omnipotent
The Lord God! Who changes not.

For Generations to Come

Our family tree
means more to me,
Than silver or gold, or a
Rolls Royce.

I can rejoice and be glad,
that Mother and Dad loved each other—
and God
Who blessed their union.

From one to another, we are linked
    to each other . . .
Through the blessings and mercy or our awesome
    Creator

Our Creator, the Artist, Who reminds us of
Eternity

In the smiles of our children, who have the
Spirit of our ancestors—
Twinkling out from their eyes . . .

Reminding us
of
Generations to come.

SJ Forevermore

SJ, today
You lift me up.

Yesterday, you filled my cup.
Tomorrow and forevermore,
You are my keys to heaven's door.

Praise to
Father
Son
and Spirit.
Thanks, S.J.,
Forever.

P.S. Thanks for breaking bonds and curses.
Sunshine feels real good.

Beloved,

Is the moon ashamed of the glory of the sun?
Is the believer ashamed of the gospel of Jesus Christ?
I count it an honor and a privilege to know you and be a part of your life.
Your strength, your wisdom, the beauty of your spirit are like spring rain to my soul.
Forgive the frailties of my human spirit. The iniquities that plague my DNA if you will.
Love, eternal love that is, overcomes obstacles. You are my heart's desire, and I expect
that God will move mightily in our lives. May God's strength be yours, His will your
will. My prayers and my love are with you always, even before the foundations of the
world, we truly were in God's plan. I love you.
Never forget or doubt for a single second, that I love you, even as I love our heavenly
father who has ordained that we would meet and love and encourage each other. I
await all things in joy, anticipation, and patience.

Thank You

Thank you ladies and gentlemen, for reading this book, for spending time with me this way. Thanks also for your testimonies. God has planted His purpose in every one of us. May yours be fulfilled to the greatest extent.

Share this message everywhere you go:

"For God so loved the world, that He gave His only begotten Son, that whosoever believes on Him shall not perish, but shall have everlasting life." John 3:16

May God Bless You richly,
Alveda King